BUYING SAMIR

India's Street Kids

Capturing Jasmina
Buying Samir

India's Street Kids: Book 2

KIMBERLY RAE

journey**forth**®

Greenville, South Carolina

Library of Congress Cataloging-in Publication Data
Rae, Kimberly, author.
    Buying Samir / Kimberly Rae.
        pages cm. — (India's street kids ; book 2)
    Summary: "Jasmina searches for her brother Samir only to
learn he is working for their former captors. Jasmina's attempt to
rescue a group of girls puts all their lives in danger"— Provided by
publisher.
    ISBN 978-1-60682-952-3 (perfect bound pbk. : alk. paper) —
ISBN 978-1-60682-953-0 (ebook) [1. Human trafficking—Fiction.
2. Brothers and sisters—Fiction. 3. Street children—Fiction. 4.
India—Fiction.] I. Title.
    PZ7.R1231Buy 2014
    [Fic]—dc23

                                                        2014024333

Cover Photo: iStockphoto.com © Vardhan (Indian boy)

Design by Nathan Hutcheon
Page layout by Michael Boone

© 2014 by BJU Press
Greenville, South Carolina 29614
JourneyForth Books is a division of BJU Press

Printed in the United States of America

ISBN 978-1-60682-952-3
eISBN 978-1-60682-953-0

15   14   13   12   11   10   9   8   7   6   5   4   3   2   1

To Shawne Ebersole

with thanks for shining your light over my life and the lives of so many others, big and small, on both sides of the world.

Ye have plowed wickedness,
ye have reaped iniquity;
ye have eaten the fruit of lies . . .

Hosea 10:13

contents

Prologue

I may die tomorrow.

He says there is no danger. I have two things called kidneys inside me, and I only need one. He says I will be paid all the money I need.

However, I have learned not to believe what a trafficker says.

Even if the trafficker is my brother.

Sleep is impossible. Pesky, loud mosquitoes invade my room. But worse, memories invade my mind. So many wrong choices.

I ran away to find my brother, and I succeeded. I sacrificed to free him, my first step toward putting my family back together, and in that I failed. Now here I am, waiting to sell a part of myself to someone who packages pieces of people in boxes filled with ice to ship them across the sea.

My body shakes. I am terrified. If I die tomorrow, what will happen to me? The girl in the room beside mine is selling a kidney to pay her mother's doctor bills. She said the gods would look favorably upon us. She is certain she will be reborn in a higher form, as a male and free to make her own choices in life.

My motivation is far less lofty. Will the gods think me bad and have me reborn as a dog, condemned to scavenge the streets, kicked aside and cursed through another lifetime of worthlessness?

If Asha were here, she would help me. She rescued me once and welcomed me into her family. I know she would want to rescue me again. But she is not here, and I can never let her see my face again. Never beg my chosen sister to tell me more of her Jesus who loves everyone—who forgives.

Tonight my thoughts, my fear, will give me no peace. So I shall write. Today when the taxi stopped at this building, I noticed a half-burned notebook in a pile of trash near the road. It was once used by a schoolgirl rich enough to discard it and buy another. I took it and shall fill it with my story.

I shall write this night, and Asha's Jesus who sees all things can read my words.

May He grant me mercy.

The Truth

Dear Mother,

Solitude is my friend tonight. The world sleeps while I write, and the silence gives comfort sleep cannot. Most nights I have nightmares of the day Father sold me or of the littered patch of sand where our home used to be. Some nights I dream of my second family, of Asha, and of Mr. Mark with his yellow hair and teeth whiter even than his white skin, and of baby Adiya. Those dreams are not frightening, only sad.

Four long years have passed since you and I lived together in the little bamboo hut by the sea. I remember helping you cook over the fire with the salty air that seasoned our food and the smell of fish that soaked into our hair and clothes and never washed out. I can hear the soft music of your voice in a whisper as you used to read our one book over and over to me and then taught me to read by it those hours Father was away fishing. You used to tell me to hide my intelligence, for no man would want to marry a woman smarter than himself, even if we could afford to arrange a marriage to a man from an educated family.

Do you remember, Mother? I said that was not fair, and you reminded me that all life was suffering, and good karma would come if we accepted our fates without complaint.

I stopped believing that. I was certain I could fight my fate, change things. My plan was so simple. I would find Samir and set him free and then together we would find and free you and Father. That ideal was as sweet and alluring as the Coca-Cola sold in glass bottles at the stall across the street from this building. Earlier today I watched a schoolboy pull rupees from his pocket and trade them for one of those bottles. The seller popped the cap off, inserted a straw, and then handed the bottle to the boy. In eleven seconds—I counted—the drink was gone, and the boy was left with nothing in his hands but an empty bottle.

Yes, my hope was as sweet as that drink and as easily consumed.

Right now I sit on one of three woven mats laid out across a concrete floor in a room so small the mats overlap each other. A girl sleeps on the green mat spread along the wall opposite me. The small blue mat wedged between lies vacant. Kiya, the girl who slept there, was called to the operating room nearly an hour ago. She looked brave as she rose to go, her unfocused eyes without fear. Samir told me they put drugs in every patient's meal beforehand to relax them. I think the real purpose of the sedation is to keep us too lethargic to run away as the danger gets closer.

I know he put a sedative in my meal tonight, but I traded meals with the other girl in my room. She had been crying since she arrived. Her operation is scheduled the day after mine, but now she sleeps so hard I keep checking her breathing to see if she is still alive. A hard ball of guilt fills my stomach, but I could not bear to spend this last night listening to her sobs, even if what I did does put me on the same level as Samir. What is one more sin added to a pile of so many?

If this operation tomorrow is successful, I will have enough money to come find you and buy your freedom. If it is not, I am determined Samir must bring this book to you. He will not want to, but I will make him promise. And since he never did learn to read, I need not fear expressing my deepest thoughts . . . or the truth about him.

Mother, Samir is a trafficker. He has become what he hates. I gave up everything to try to rescue him, only to find him no longer a slave to cruel masters but a slave to his own greed for money and lust for revenge.

You will want to know how this happened. To tell you I must go back to when we arrived on the compound two days before my second family left India . . . without me.

two

A Rescue

"It's a sari shop rescue, and we need you to wait behind the secret panel."

Mr. Mark, Asha's yellow-haired American husband, had just parked inside the compound gate when Amrita approached regally with those words. I had seen Amrita once or twice since I came to live with Asha, and every time her beauty stunned me. Thick eyebrows arched high over long, dark eyelashes, oval-shaped eyes, and skin as smooth as cream. Her makeup was a work of art, her nails perfectly manicured, her arms covered in bangles. I did not know how she came to work with Asha, but she was the perfect person to run a hair and beauty salon near the red-light district, listening for word of women and girls who wanted to escape. "You were supposed to be here hours ago," she said.

Asha stepped out of the Land Rover, one hand holding baby Adiya, the other clutching a plastic bag against her stomach. "I got sick," she said. "The roads are bumpy and the traffic so swervy, I—"

Her face went pale. She thrust Adiya into Amrita's arms and leaned over to heave the rest of her breakfast into the bag.

I stayed in the back seat and swallowed to keep my own churning stomach from following her example. Mark had needed to stop the vehicle four times on our trip, stretching the normally two-hour drive to the compound into a long four.

"Are you contagious?"

I looked out the open back-seat window and had to smile. Amrita stood holding Adiya out from her as if the baby was a vial of germs. "Don't spit up on my outfit," she warned, looking over Adiya's chubby legs and arms and then with a grimace at her mouth when the baby gurgled. "Is she going to throw up? I have to be at the shop in an hour to do this rescue."

Asha finished and stood upright. Mr. Mark handed her a tissue from a little compartment in front of the passenger seat and held out his hand for the bag. He must love her very much to do for her what only a servant would do. "The baby isn't sick," she said, wiping her mouth as her husband walked away with the bag and then taking Adiya from Amrita, who released her without objection. "And neither am I. At least I wasn't until this morning. Must have been that curried shrimp we had last night with the—"

She suddenly handed Adiya back to me—I had opened the door and stepped out—and ran toward some bushes along the compound wall. Amrita looked at the baby, then at me. "You'd fit in the secret panel," she said. "Asha is in no condition to go on this rescue. If she threw up and gave away the location of the secret room, it would mess up everything. Do you want to help rescue a new girl tonight?"

I couldn't speak. Did she mean it, or was she just talking around an idea like adults sometimes did before they remembered they were speaking with a child?

Amrita eyed me. "You're young, but if you can handle closed dark spaces and keep quiet, I'll take you with me." She added, "There isn't anybody else small enough except Dapika."

She did not need to voice why Dapika, the only girl on the compound around my age, had not been presented with this opportunity. What sang of adventure to me was painful memory to her. I thought back to my previous visit, the day I had gotten angry at Dapika and mocked her coward's heart. In truth I spoke out in jealousy over her easy ability to get people to like her, something I do not have. She told me why she vowed to never go near that district again. It was not the dangers she feared, but the reminders of her life there with her mother before they were rescued.

No, Amrita would not even ask her. I was her only option.

I bounced Adiya on my hip, focusing on her to keep my punctured pride from showing. "When do we leave?" I asked.

"As soon as we can get the baby to somebody who can hold her longer than five minutes." Her gaze pointed to Asha, who left the bushes and headed for the guard's small dwelling near the compound gate. The guard, Milo's father, exited the front door with a tin bucket held out toward Asha's green-tinged face.

Amrita took my elbow and led me toward one of the six houses inside the compound walls. "Let's take the baby to Mark's grandmother and then we can go before Asha recovers enough to find out where you're going and says you can't."

I decided I liked Amrita.

Three

A Secret Room

I had not been to Kolkata's notorious red-light district since the day Milo, Dapika, and I rescued baby Adiya from that terrible madam. Little had changed. The same dirty, graffiti-covered buildings rose like castles of evil, surrounded by moats of garbage and sewage. Indian music from one roadside stall competed with a Chinese tune across the street. Women stood in lines, their faces painted, their outfits bright, and their eyes empty.

I had forgotten how despair hung like a cloud of pollution over that part of the city.

We rode in a rickshaw past the worst section and onto a narrow road nearby. Shadows fought the fading light and made the buildings appear to lean down over the street, covering and closing in on me.

A sigh of relief escaped my lips when the rickshaw stopped in front of a small sari shop. The window revealed one tattered mannequin draped in yards of purple silk.

"This is the place," Amrita said, her voice low. "Hurry."

I slipped down and rushed inside.

"Not like that," she barked. "The idea is to not draw attention to yourself. Act normal."

As I had never been inside a sari store, I had little idea of what normal behavior was. I gawked at the folded saris displayed along the walls, some in stacks and some draped over rows of wooden rods.

"Beautiful," I breathed out.

"Yes, yes. They're pretty. Keep moving." Amrita put her palms together then touched them to her forehead to greet a young man working in the shop. He returned the gesture. I did as well, but he was already looking out onto the street and did not see.

"Is my order ready?" Amrita asked.

The man, still looking outside, gave a slight nod. "She needs to be measured," he said.

For a moment, I let myself pretend I really was there to be fitted. I pictured myself draped in the glorious purple sari embroidered in gold.

A door opened at the back of the shop, and another young man beckoned to us.

"Go." Amrita nudged me and I crossed the small area to the door. The man ushered us inside, and I found myself in a tiny room—the measuring room, Amrita called it. "It connects the sari shop and tailor shop." The man exited the room. In the small stream of light that entered while the door was open, I saw Amrita pull on a section of the wooden paneling. It turned out to be a secret door.

"Come." She motioned. The door to the tailor shop closed, and we were encased in darkness, as if we'd been thrown into a black river and the dark water swirled around me. I felt my way toward Amrita. When a hand grasped my shoulder, I nearly screamed.

"Shh." Her hand guided me to the tiny space behind the open panel. I had to kneel to crawl inside. Amrita whispered instructions and then shut me in, alone.

The darkness was thick and heavy in the small space. I labored to breath and pulled my knees up to my chest. I started listing the names of gods and goddesses, hoping I did not accidentally repeat a name and anger the others. I even called on Asha's Jesus.

The panel creaked, and I pulled my knees in tight to make room, and to contain my trembling. I heard Amrita whisper and then something, a leg or arm, brushed against me. Had it been the eight legs of a huge furry spider, I could not have been more afraid.

However, my instructions had been clear. *Help the rescued girl not to panic while you wait.*

Amrita had told me what to do. She had not told me how.

Waiting

"Don't be scared," I whispered, wondering if the girl noticed that my teeth chattered as I said it. "We only have to wait here until they are sure no one followed you or is searching for you, and then they will take you to the House of Hope. It's a safe place outside the city with rice fields and trees and chickens. You'll like it."

The girl shifted, and in the cramped space I could sense she was smaller than I. Her rapid breaths filled the space with soft sounds of terror. In. Out. In. Out. I felt my own fear grow.

"How old are you?" I asked.

It sounded as if a mouse whispered back. "Twelve."

Two years younger than my fourteen. At least I think I am fourteen now. I shivered. "How did you get sold?"

I waited through long moments until she spoke. "The monsoons this year were bad for rice crops, and we lost our field. My parents had nothing to sell to buy food." The girl breathed. In. Out. I leaned closer to hear. "Except one of us children."

12

I turned to face the girl, though I could not see her, and said, "My father sold my brother and me."

She sighed and continued. "There are seven of us, and I am the oldest. It was my duty to take on work so the others could live. When the man came to our village offering jobs in the city, it seemed perfect." Another silence. This time I heard my own breathing.

"I was brought to a big house but was not a paid servant as promised. They beat me and made me slave from dawn till past dark. Their house had seven empty rooms, but I had to live on a mattress in the garage. I could eat only the scraps they left on their plates and was never allowed out of the house, not even into the yard. They didn't want anyone to know I existed."

"How did you get here?"

The girl shifted again. My tailbone began to hurt. "One day I broke a plate, and the master was beating me. I looked out the window and saw a man walking down the road. I ran outside and yelled for help, but the master grabbed me by the hair and dragged me back inside. After that people must have started asking questions, because the master sold me to a factory owner from India."

I felt her shoulder shrug next to mine, but it shook with fear. "On the way across the border between Bangladesh and India, I saw a woman with a sign that said, 'Are you here against your will?' I looked at her until she looked back, and I tried to nod while the man was busy showing our papers to the border patrol. She must have understood for she followed us here. As soon as I was put into a room, she was at the window telling me this plan. She said that sometimes they can rescue girls at the border but that day the border patrol included corrupt men the traffickers had bribed."

Now I was shaking. "How did—"

Footsteps outside the panel door silenced us. I tried to keep strong but didn't object when the girl edged closer and clasped my arm.

The panel yanked open, and I squinted against the harsh beam coming from a flashlight.

"It's time. Let's go."

I recognized Amrita's voice and scrambled out of our dark box, the girl behind me. Amrita opened the door leading back to the sari shop. Opposite that door another woman I did not recognize stood in the doorway leading to the tailor shop. "Take your time getting your order before you two leave together," Amrita told her and then motioned to me. I followed her back through the saris out onto the street and to the waiting rickshaw.

My heart pounded all the way.

Five
In Trouble

We walked toward the cheerful house belonging to Eleanor Stephens, Asha's grandmother-in-law, myself certain that much trouble would be waiting when we got inside.

I was right. Asha, who considers herself my *Didi*—my big sister—fretted with words about safety and getting permission and not running off to dangerous places without telling anyone. She threw her hands around as she paced back and forth in the room decorated for entertaining guests.

I bit my lips closed and stood with my hands clasped, my eyes down in respect, but Amrita seemed unfazed. She shot out a few clipped sentences of explanation, reminded Asha that I wasn't really her sister, and then left to take the newly rescued girl to the safe house.

Asha stared at the door Amrita had shut. Her mouth opened, but no words came out. I clicked my tongue against the roof of my mouth in sympathy for my Didi. Asha had rescued so many girls, and those she rescued she protected like a lioness, which was appreciated by frightened young cubs such as Dapika, but proved difficult with fierce ones such as Amrita and me. Our gratitude for freedom showed itself in a burning desire to spread it, but anything that burns causes pain if kept too close.

"Remember, dear, these women did not grow up in a system of trusted authority as you did," Eleanor Stephens said. She held Adiya on her lap in a strange chair with curved bottom legs that tipped the chair back and forth. I kept watching, worried the chair would topple over, but it never did. "They have had to fight to survive on their own and therefore naturally have a higher degree of independence."

"I know. I've gotten used to Amrita's ways . . . almost." Asha dropped down onto a couch and sighed, gesturing toward me. "But how I can go to America for six whole weeks if I'm worried Jasmina will be running headlong into danger every other day?"

My gaze swung to the elderly woman, who smiled. "You mean like you did when you first came?"

Asha looked at Mrs. Stephens and then chuckled, and my shoulders relaxed. My heart, however, dropped at the mention of her trip—the reason I would be spending the summer months here on the compound without my protecting lioness. Long as Asha's lectures were, I soaked in the intention behind them, the value it gave me to know someone wanted me safe and cared about what happened to me. Her concern was a balm over my fear that it was somehow my fault my real family was scattered and broken.

Yet now Asha, Mr. Mark, and baby Adiya were going halfway across the world to America to see Asha's American parents, and Mr. Mark also talked about going to churches to share about their work. I did not know what work he spoke of, perhaps the trips to villages he often made or the many papers and books he seemed to constantly be translating into Bangla. All I knew was they were leaving me behind for rich relatives and fancy places with whole stores full of nothing but shoes. Away from the heat and smell of Kolkata, India.

Away from me.

"I wish you could come with us," Asha had said the day she told me of their trip, "but we can't take you out of the country without your parents' permission. And since we haven't found them yet . . . not to mention not being able to get you a passport without your birth certificate or some kind of identification . . ."

Only two things kept me from begging them to let me come. The first was that their six weeks gone fit into something Asha called summer break, and I would not have to go to school or study. The second, and most important, was that Mrs. Stephens had agreed to help me search for Samir. She already had several of the city's quarries marked on a map.

I could not have enjoyed America's abundance knowing he was out there, a slave, probably abused and lonely. I had to stay and find him, to help him escape. Even so, when the three people who had become my new family left later that week, though I watched them depart without tears, I cried inside.

I was alone again.

Hot Water

Early Sunday morning I awoke with the sun and looked around my room in Eleanor Stephen's home. I lay still, moving only my eyes, thinking of my past and comparing this room to my childhood home near the sea.

The walls in this house were concrete, much more solid and strong than the bamboo that made up our one-room hut. No cracks to let in the sweltering heat or the chill of the cold months. No bamboo to attract bugs or thatch on the roof to cave in on my head like the time a large rat tried to run across it. The floor was cool, hard tile rather than packed dirt; the windows were screened and barred, protection against predators of every size. In our hut we'd had a window; it was simply a section of the bamboo wall cut out for air. It had no screening of any kind, leaving us susceptible to hungry bugs and sometimes larger creatures. A thief could have utilized the window, but coming through the doorway would have been easier, and what did we have worth stealing anyway? Our one cooking pot?

My eyes shut tight as I recalled the nightmare that woke me. It was always the same: my father's face as he took the money; my brother's face as we were pulled away; my mother's fading features, her image blurry to my memory.

A thief did come through the front door of our home. He stole me.

No, he bought me, which is worse. Had he kidnapped me, at least I could have known the false hope that my parents were searching for me, missing me, wanting me home. What did I have now?

A rooster crowed outside and startled a small gecko on the window screen. It climbed up to the ceiling and then scurried across to hide above the fan. I might as well get up. I gathered my blue *shalwar kameez* pants, top, and *orna* into my arms, along with a brush to do something about the wild mess of my hair, and sneaked toward Grandmother's room. "Everyone on the compound calls me Grandmother," Eleanor Stephens had told me, so I had begun to call her that as well.

I was going to take a shower.

It's a phrase the Americans use—*take a shower*—that means they go into a tiny square inside a bathroom and stand under a waterfall that turns on and off. Asha and Mark have one at their house, but I was never brave enough to try it. What if I drowned?

Even so, the concept of water raining down on me tugged at my curiosity until I determined to try it. I had two hours, since Grandmother and everyone else on the compound had gone to church. I had gotten out of going by saying my stomach hurt and I needed to stay close to the bathroom. That's another phrase Americans like—*stay close to the bathroom* or *my stomach is not agreeing with me*. These are softer ways of saying what spicy Indian food can do to one's digestion. For Americans, at times it seems more polite to not say what is really going on.

I hesitated in the doorway of Grandmother's room. Her bed was made, a light-colored quilt folded neatly and draped over the edge. Her walls were lined with old, faded photographs. There was one shelf with candles on candlesticks for frequent power outages and another shelf on the far wall above her bed.

It was that shelf that pulled me into the room. I treaded softly though that was silly since no one was home, but I had never been inside her room before. At first I thought the shelf held small stone people like the shelf in the main visiting room, but as I got closer I saw the statues were not people but animals. Strange ones I had never seen. They must be the kind of animals that live in America. One little one had a black stripe across his face, as if he were a thief wearing a mask. I picked it up and studied it, smiling.

A noise from the front of the house jolted me so I almost dropped the little animal. I quickly returned it to its perch on the shelf and rushed to the bathroom, closing the door behind me. Maybe the guard had left the gate and come to check on me. If he heard the water running, would he tell?

Quickly and quietly, I dropped my clothes, both the ones I carried and the ones I was wearing, onto the floor near the small shower box and dropped my brush next to them. I stepped inside and wondered what to do next. A curtain hung at the edge of the tiled box area. Should I pull it so it closed me inside? What would be the purpose of that? No, that would get the curtain wet and then Grandmother would know I had been there.

I looked on the wall in front of me and saw several knobs to pull or push or turn. Which one sent the water out? I touched several before deciding to start with the knob on the right and got blasted with ice cold water.

"Ahhhhhhhh!" It was no waterfall. It was a monsoon. In winter!

I didn't know how to make it stop. I turned another knob, which at first only made more water shoot out at me, but then the water turned warm. Then hot, too hot.

"Ahhhhhhhh!" I screamed again, but this time in pain. I couldn't find any other knobs to turn. I hopped around and then jumped out of the shower and my right foot landed on my brush. "Ouch!"

I opened the bathroom door and ran from the scalding water. Halfway across the room, I jerked to a stop.

Grandmother stood in the doorway. Her eyes went huge. "Jasmina! What on earth?"

"Ahhhhhhhh!" It must have been my day for screaming. I turned and ran back into the bathroom and slammed the door behind me. Oh, horrors. What would she think of me, running naked through her house like some barbarian child?

The hot water had filled the entire bathroom with steam. My clothes were soaked. I picked them up, but doing so brought me into the water's path, and I screamed again.

"Jasmina, for goodness' sake, what are you doing in there? Why do you have the water running full blast?"

"I can't turn it off!" I yelled, utterly humiliated. "It's hot and burning me!"

"Come out this instant, child." I heard through the door. "I've got my eyes closed. Go into your room and get dressed. I'll take care of the water."

I didn't want her to get burned, so I stood still for several seconds, trying to decide what to do. I was covered in sweat from the hot steam. When it became hard to breathe, I opened the door. Ah, relief. The air outside the bathroom, which had felt stale and hot earlier, at that moment was a cool breeze on my skin. I was relieved to see Grandmother had her back to me. I darted across the room and then across the hallway after one quick look out the window at the end to make sure the guard wasn't standing there looking in. Why he would be, I didn't know, but then why was Grandmother suddenly in her house instead of at church?

And what excuse could I come up with to explain sneaking in to use her shower?

seven
Questions

Nothing good came to mind. I considered saying I got a cut or a burn and thought the water would help, but that was ridiculous. The dipper bath I usually used would be fine for that.

There really wasn't any option other than telling the truth.

"I was curious," I said once I got dressed and sat across from Grandmother at the dining room table. I tried not to remember her seeing me without my clothes on. I clasped my hands in my lap and did not look at her. "I wanted to know what it was like."

"Well, that's fine, dear, but why didn't you just ask me?"

Why didn't I just ask? I dared a look up. Had she lived in India so long but still not learned our Indian ways? I lowered my eyes. "I don't know."

"Hmm." Grandmother retreated to the kitchen, and I sat still, imagining all the punishments she would inflict upon me. How could I do such a thing my first week in her home? I had abused her hospitality, a deeply insulting offense. I remembered back to my childhood, the day I was nearly swept out to sea. I had chased a fish, wanting to find its home, and had not noticed the tide until it swept me from my feet. Father had caught me that day and pulled me to shore, swearing and shouting that curiosity was deadly.

When Grandmother returned, two cups of a wonderful American drink called hot chocolate in her hands, I blurted out my thoughts. "How do you stand it?"

"Stand what?"

I took the offered cup, angry at my foolish bravery in voicing questions when I should have kept my head bowed in silent shame. "The shower. All that hard water hurts, and it's so cold it freezes, then so hot it burns. It's horrible."

Grandmother put the cup to her lips, but it did not hide the fact that she was smiling. "You turn the knobs different ways for different levels of cold and hot. And you also get to choose how much pressure you want the water to have, so the shower can be comfortable rather than horrible."

Dipper baths were much simpler. Put the dipper in the water. Pour the water over yourself. "Oh," was all I said.

"That is why, if you want to try something new or learn about something, you should ask someone."

"Oh," I said again.

Grandmother sighed. "Sometimes I forget that you have been on your own for so long. Most of our orphans came at very young ages and do not have such a need to discover everything independently. They are not afraid to ask about what they do not know."

Afraid? Did she not know it is unthinkable for someone of my status, not to mention my age, to presume to ask questions or be curious? We are to obey, fulfill our duties, and hope our karma comes to rest in a good place for it. It is not fear, but good manners.

Grandmother set down her cup. "Well, for now, let's leave the shower and get to the real reason I came back today."

Leave the shower? Neither of us was in the shower anymore. I wondered what she meant, and then the rest of her words sank in. "Why did you come back today?"

She took another sip of her drink. "All the way to church, my own stomach was bothering me. I kept thinking of you and wondering if you were okay, so I decided to come back and check to see if you needed some medicine or a trip to the doctor."

At that I did bow my head in shame. She had been so kind, and I had repaid her with deceit. I considered dropping to my knees to touch my hand to her feet and then my head and heart in *pronam*, a sincere gesture of humility and apology, but every time I'd seen it done with a Westerner, it seemed to make them vastly uncomfortable. Asha once told me they preferred words said aloud, but just the thought of being so direct made me the vastly uncomfortable one. I sighed.

"Now." Her voice held no reproach, and I looked up, surprised to see that smile still shining on her elderly face. I wondered how old she was. It was hard to tell with white people. "Since your stomach seems to have recovered . . ." She chuckled, and my face flamed. "Instead of getting medicine, how about we make ourselves a plan for finding that brother of yours?"

eight
A Second Letter

Dear Mother,

Sometimes I do not understand the missionaries. They walk a different path. Asha says it is the path of God. They believe in being kind to everyone, and they ignore the status lines that border and define all people. They give without hidden motives. They pray as if God actually listens to them and cares about what they need.

You are surely ashamed of your daughter after reading how presumptuous I was in taking a shower. You will be much more ashamed at what you read later. But Grandmother was not angry. Not even sad. She seemed to think it funny.

I will describe her for you. She is old, and her skin is white and thin as paper. When she laughs, which is often, lines crinkle up near her eyes. Her hair curls around her head in a white cloud. She likes to go for walks in the cool of the evening and wears ornas around her shoulders to keep warm.

Her house is vast and luxurious compared to ours, but she says it is small compared to most homes where she comes from. Her room for guests is filled with fluffy, lacy items I cannot define. The table for eating is covered in a cloth, but then the cloth is covered in smaller cloths in front of each seat. I think the table must be broken, and so she is covering it up. When I first arrived, she had miniature people on her shelves. They did not look like any idols I had ever seen, and there were no incense sticks to burn. I knew I should not be rude and ask questions, but the mystery puzzled me.

I miss so much about her. Her purple umbrella that she used to ward off sunshine as well as rain. Her hot chocolate. Her worn Bible so old some of the pages had begun to crumble, and her gentle voice reading aloud from it each night. Her simple prayers and her kindness to fellow missionary and orphan alike. She treated everyone as if they had value. Even me.

We planned to begin our search for Samir the following morning. She had marked five quarries on her map and drew our route from the nearest to the farthest. I was glad to have her help as we planned, but feared her presence would not be an asset as I searched. She was so very white, which would draw attention, and so very old, which would slow me down. And what would she do if we found the right quarry and I needed to sneak in to ask questions? I knew that if she followed, they would never forget her face, and we would both be put in danger.

I preferred to go on my own, but she would not consider that idea. That night as I lay in bed, I thought of you and Father. I wondered if you were somewhere thinking of me. I decided if I were able to find Samir and rescue him, Father would surely want us back. Certain that if I worked hard enough, I would be able to put our family back together again.

And now you will be sad, for we both know I was wrong.

nine
One Million Children

Morning came and I dragged my sleepy body across the floor toward the wardrobe where three shalwar kameez outfits awaited my choice. One was red with white embroidery, one was a faded brown, and the third was my blue one, not quite dry after its soak in the shower the day earlier.

I chose the red. It was an important day.

After breakfast Grandmother led the way across the compound and out toward the street, umbrella open to shade her from the harsh sun. The gate swung shut behind me, and I looked around at a chaotic world of rickshaws, *autos*, taxis, pedestrians, a few sacred cows—sacred to Hindus, that is, which is nearly everyone in the country—and several more not-sacred goats and chickens.

This was the day I had waited for. Rather than the expected excitement, I found myself frozen in fear. Would we find him? Would he be willing to risk escape?

About a million children worked the quarries. Grandmother told me that statistic as we climbed into the auto. A million. And that was just in India. How would I find one among so many? The auto neared the first quarry on our list, and I looked across the vast expanse of rock, mountains of stone with no tree or anything green or growing in sight, as if an earthquake had shaken a massive tomb and crumbled it to pieces.

And then the dead came to life. A cluster of forms rose above a large pile. Through the hazy fog of stone dust appeared children, all grey—grey metal buckets, grey stone, grey skin, hair, lips. Only the eyes reassured me they were not ghosts, but real living children. Had I looked like that?

"Oh, heavenly Father, deliver these precious children from evil." She spoke with her eyes on the children, but I knew Grandmother was praying.

My eyes stung, and I wiped at them. "The dust is getting in my eyes," I said and looked away.

Grandmother took my arm, and we walked together toward a small building at the base of the largest mound of rock. "It's bad enough that adults have to work in places like this. How horrible when their children have to work as well."

I was already shaking my head, not thinking of the plight of those families but rather the plight that was once my own. "This isn't the right quarry. Ours had only children."

"Would you want to talk with someone to see if we can get more information on the other quarries? Perhaps narrow them down?"

The front door of the building opened, and a man emerged. Though we remained at a distance, I saw his face clearly enough to know he was not the one who trafficked me. I also saw, as he stared with calculated focus, that we should not ask him even one question.

I turned to Grandmother and put as much urgency in my voice as I could, hoping her insight would receive what I could not yet fully communicate. "We need to go. Now."

She looked at me for two long seconds and then nodded and immediately turned away from the building and back toward the waiting auto. Once inside and back on the road, she asked me to explain.

"I got a terrible feeling. I don't know why. I just knew we had to leave before he could talk with us or get a good look at our faces."

Her lips pursed together. "Were you afraid he would harm you?"

"No." I watched the traffic flow around us and tried to form an answer that made sense. "I have this feeling deep inside that the men in power are connected somehow. I'm afraid if we go right in and ask questions, we may not get the information in time. Word will spread, and something terrible will happen to Samir before we reach him."

To my surprise, Grandmother nodded. "Yes, I see your point. We know from personal experience that the connections between traffickers run deep and can be deadly." She glanced at me and her look held respect. "From now on, we will consider ourselves *incognito*."

She often slipped a few English words into our conversations, knowing I had been studying the foreign language with Asha. Sometimes I wondered if she had used both languages for so long, she forgot which was which. This word was new to me. Long and complicated. My eyebrows went up and she smiled. "Secret, like spies."

Her voice sounded young and fresh. "By the way," she added, a twinkle in her eye, "many years ago, when my husband and I first married and we lived in a village far from here, I once rescued a woman from *suttee*."

Her words were a welcome distraction.

"She was going to be buried alive?"

"Yes." She frowned and then giggled. "I hid her in the kitchen cupboards under my sink. Stood right in front of the sink while the men searched the house." She looked at me and smiled. "Back in my day, I was much like you. You'll find being old, like being a child, means those who love you want to protect you, sometimes more than you want to be protected." She patted my shoulder, then squeezed it with affection. "I do believe with our main protectors away today, we shall have ourselves an adventure."

ten
The Men

We rode to the next quarry on Grandmother's list, trying to think of some kind of strategy that would enable us to get information without revealing ourselves. From the entrance to the second quarry, I could easily see this was not the one Samir and I were taken to by the man with the smooth smile—the man who himself never got close enough to the stones to encounter a speck of dust. "This isn't the one."

I was shaking my head when I saw them. Immediately I pulled back inside the auto, curling my body as close into the corner of the seat as possible. As attention-grabbing as Grandmother's white skin was, I still used her as a human shield, pulling her forward on the seat until her body hid the presence of mine. I shook more violently than the girl behind the secret panel had.

"What is it?" Grandmother was instantly on alert.

"It's him. It's both of them." Even my voice shook.

How was it possible? The smooth man, the one who found us after the garment factory fire and offered us a job, who brought us to the quarry and without apology forced us into slave labor, walked alongside the gate to the quarry. Next to him was a man I had hoped to never see again. The garment factory owner. The man who introduced me to trafficking as a child.

What were they doing together?

Though I had added no information to my earlier statement, Grandmother gave the next address to the driver, and we pulled away from the quarry before I could beg her to take us far from both men. And beg I would have. Desperately.

After a mile or two, I found my voice. "They must work together. I wonder if they knew each other back when—" My mind saw the garment factory, the foot-pedal sewing machines, the fire consuming them all. Had the quarry owner known about the fire? Was he out looking for vulnerable kids like Samir and me? Had he started the fire? "Maybe the garment factory owner found out the quarry owner has Samir and is there to get him back."

If the smooth man was in charge of more than one quarry, how would I ever find my brother? He could be in any of them, or already in another garment factory.

I moaned and put my head into my hands.

As we rode, I told Grandmother about the garment factory owner, the fat-bellied man who locked me away at night so I would not escape, the man who trapped me in a windowless building sweating over other people's clothing for three long years. Grandmother's face hardened as I spoke. Her eyes remained forward on the road, her eyebrows pinched together. She gave a word to the driver, and he pulled over on the busy street. Ignoring the vendors, swerving rickshaws, and honking autos, she closed her eyes and began to pray out loud.

I looked around, self-conscious, but when her words were on my behalf, words of anger against the evil done to me and my family, I stopped caring what anyone might think of the strange white woman praying. I focused on her mouth as it moved into words asking God to help me. Me. She was praying for *me*.

I peeked out the window and looked up, expecting a sign that her God was listening. A buzzard flew over my head. Surely that was not my sign, unless it was a bad omen. Maybe God was saying that I was not worth praying for.

A soft hand gripped my arm and I jumped, banging my head against the window frame. "Ow!"

"Sorry, dear. I didn't mean to scare you."

Scare me? Little about Grandmother could be considered frightening. No, what was frightening was the risk of my brother's traffickers capturing me again. I had seen escaped kids caught and taken into Gar's "office." Whatever punishment he gave them was so horrible, none of them ever had the courage to try a second time.

"I don't want to visit any more quarries," I said, my lips tight around my teeth. "I want to go back. This won't work. If they are working together now, Samir's situation is hopeless." As was mine.

I would never be able to rescue him. I would never be able to face my parents again.

All was lost.

The Runaways

We rode forward again despite my protests.

"Jasmina, I need to think, and as I do so, we might as well drive to the rest of the quarries on my list. There will never be a safer time, since right now we know both men are at the quarry we just left."

Her logic was sound, but not strong enough to calm my trembling. I wanted to go back to her home, climb into the soft bed in her guest room, and pull the pastel yellow blanket over my head until the fear settled into something I could handle. As it was, I fought the panicked desire to jump from the auto and run, an action I knew would be foolish. Getting lost in this city would not make me safer.

The auto stopped, and my heart stopped as well. Grandmother glanced at my face and her lips tightened into a line again. "This is the place, isn't it?"

I nodded. At that point I would have had no strength to run. My body flooded with memories: the feel of blisters on my hands bursting into raw craters; stone dust coating my hair into hard strings of grey; coughing, always coughing; longing for water, even the tiniest amount, to quench the never-ending thirst.

Which side should I listen to? The side of me that longed to rush inside and see if my brother was still there, or the side that wanted to turn and run as far from this place of horror as possible?

"Jasmina." Grandmother's whisper drew my attention more than had she shouted. I looked at her face and saw compassion and understanding. "I have an idea, but it will require much courage from you."

Curiosity overcame my fear, at least momentarily. She told me her plan, and as soon as I agreed, she asked the driver to take us in the auto through the quarry. She pulled out a camera and smiled, looking like a foreign tourist just wanting a few pictures of the famed Indian stone. The driver smiled back benevolently. Having a tourist passenger meant more money, so he did not mind her strange request.

We entered the quarry through the open gate. I knew a path wove around the mountains of stone, perfect for a photographer to take a scenic tour. The path was for machines, heavy, smoke-belching machines that took the hammered stone and sent it by the truckload to places unknown, places where people pay much money for stone to line their floors, or, as Grandmother informed me, to make designed paths in their gardens, yet another thought as foreign and strange to me as her transparent skin.

A third of the way around the quarry, three large trucks blocked our path. We were not nearly far enough in. How could I get deep enough into the mounds to be seen as a quarry slave if I could not even get near the sections where the children worked?

I stepped from the auto as the driver tried to explain in very broken English that he would not be able to get around the parked trucks. He seemed to have forgotten Grandmother had been speaking to him in Bangla this whole time. Tourists cannot speak Bangla. He gestured and pointed toward the trucks.

Grandmother saw me moving away from the auto and kept the driver's attention by asking questions using English words and her own wide gestures, repeating herself louder when he didn't understand. Despite my anxiety, I stifled a laugh. Her voice toned high and then low, and her words did not blend together into music like Bangla words do. Each word was individual, like scissor cuts across cloth, just like the American tourists I'd heard when I lived on the streets.

A few steps away from the first truck, I could not bear the tension and broke into a run. The crunch of my sandals as they pushed against the gravel beneath my feet alerted the driver. He shouted. I darted around the nearest truck, looking back to see Grandmother sigh very loudly and then speak rapidly in English, pointing toward me and shaking her head. She stepped down from the auto and was coming my way from the right when another sound came from around the truck to my left. It was the sound of gravel falling, the crunch of a thousand tiny stones as they rolled over and against each other.

Had someone seen us? Were they coming after me? My heart pounded against my chest. I breathed in and the dust coated my lungs, and I willed myself not to cough it back out. I tiptoed around the truck until I could see. The sight was so shocking I could not answer Grandmother when she called out behind me.

There, only two body lengths away, was not a predator or a trafficker.

It was a child. Two of them. Girls much younger than I. They ran toward me, terror on their faces under the layers of grey dust.

twelve
Change of Plans

"Goodness gracious. What on earth?"

I heard the words, but Grandmother spoke in English, and I had no idea what she said. The girls had nearly reached me. When they saw Grandmother, even the grey dust did not hide their pale faces. They were terrified.

Of what?

They came to a halt near me, whispering frantically. I caught something about escaping and a man, but both were talking at once. When I heard more gravel crunching, the girls ran around me to Grandmother, their fear of whatever followed behind greater than their fear of a white woman. They clung to her legs and begged her help.

"Of course I will help you," Grandmother said. "But what is wrong?"

The sound came closer. Over the hill past the farthest truck, I saw him. A young man crested the hill. Only his feet covered in dust, so he was not a quarry slave. He looked around as he ran. When he saw us, the girls screamed. Grandmother immediately grabbed them both by the arms and took off at a run toward the auto. "Turn it on!" she yelled at the driver. "Turn the engine on!"

I stared. The driver had left the engine running of course, but he shifted gears with one hand and his other clutched the steering wheel, ready to flee. Grandmother was at the vehicle, trying to lift the girls in. How had she managed to move so quickly?

"Jasmina! Help me!"

What was I doing? I stopped staring and ran. By the time I reached Grandmother, one of the girls was inside the auto. I lifted the other and flung her forward, jumping in just as the driver began a wild turn that nearly knocked me back out onto the gravel. I hung on, looking back at the ground. Both the potential pain of impact and the fear of being left stranded at the quarry turned my fingers to steel where I gripped the outsides of the open doorway.

As Grandmother pulled me to safety, I looked back in time to see the man sprinting around the largest truck. He ran toward us, yelling and waving, anger radiating from him.

"Go! Hurry!" I shouted to the driver.

We sped away, all of us breathing hard and coughing dust. "Thank God we were successful," Grandmother said. I started to agree, but then realized I had not talked to any child in the quarry or discovered even one hint about my brother's whereabouts. How was I going to get back and get the information I needed about Samir? As Grandmother said, any other time we would not know where either of the traffickers was and if it was safe to return.

This had not been a success. Not for me.

My voice was hard with disappointment and, yes, a little anger, as I turned to the two girls who cried hard beside me. "Well, who are you, and why were you running away?"

Grandmother sent a look my way, and I knew she was disappointed at my lack of compassion. Her arms wrapped around both girls' heaving shoulders, and her voice was kind as I looked out the window at the passing buildings of the city. "Children, what is it? Tell me what happened."

The girls choked and coughed. I turned and watched the tears turn the dust on their little faces into mud. The older of the two, possibly nine or ten, spoke between coughs. "Bad men. Brought us to the city. Separated us."

"They made us carry rocks all day," the younger one cried out. "If I dropped the rocks, they hit me!"

"Horrible," Grandmother said, as clearly shocked as I was not. How did she expect slaves to be treated?

"He—the man—told us today that our parents are dead." She shook her head. "But it's not true. I heard him send some guards to go after a man and woman who had escaped from the other quarry. I know it was them."

"So you were running away," Grandmother said, touching a gentle hand to the younger one's hair. She had curled up and rested her head on Grandmother's shoulder, instinctively knowing Grandmother could be trusted.

"We have to find them," the older one said.

"Then we can go home to our village again," the younger added.

"We'll do everything we can to help you," Grandmother told them. "Won't we, Jasmina?"

Questions about Samir balanced on my tongue ready to spring from my mouth, but I was silenced by the message in Grandmother's eyes. I might have been impressed with my newfound ability to read facial signals had I not recognized that the talent was hers. She had an uncanny ability to communicate without words.

So I sat silently while Grandmother reassured the girls, patted their shoulders, and then prayed for them. I knew she wanted me to feel sorry for them too, but I could not. I had learned to lock my heart against the other quarry children. Caring just meant more heartache later when they were sold away or injured or just disappeared.

I had only enough space in my heart to care about finding my brother, and all my hopes of finding him that day got left behind in the quarry dust.

The girls continued to cry. I sulked all the way back to the compound.

thirteen
The Village

Most of the night my mind tossed and turned like a fish flung onto the sand. Back and forth, seeking a solution. I had to help my brother, but Grandmother's presence with me on the search could only end in failure. If I discovered Samir and we needed to run, she could never keep up, and what might they do to her? I could not put her in such danger. I would have to leave and find him on my own.

The question was how? How could I get out without her knowing?

Morning came too soon. I stepped outside Grandmother's home, and my gaze circled the area until it stopped at the orphanage building. Milo came through the front door, sat on the porch steps, and waved to where his father guarded the compound gate. Milo wore his usual stained white shirt with the pocket half-falling off. He was always happiest when he dressed like the street kid he used to be. He set his crutch against the wall behind him. Below his shorts, ragged at the edges, he rubbed the spot where his one leg abruptly ended in a small knob where a foot should have been. As I approached,

I saw how his eyebrows came together, and I wondered if his leg hurt.

Milo was the first person I met when Asha brought me to the compound, and he was one of the few people in the world to show me unrestrained acceptance. I considered him my friend. When he looked up, I glanced away so he would not know I had been staring. I did not think he would like the idea that I felt sorry for him.

By the time I looked back his way, he was sitting up, no trace of pain on his face, proving I had been right. "Hi." His smile lit up his face. It was no wonder he used to get free ice cream when he lived on the streets. Though typically not quick to smile, my mouth curved upward in response. "How did it go today? Did you find the right quarry?" he asked.

I nodded, my smile melting into a frown.

"Did you see your brother?"

I heard Dapika's voice before I saw her behind the screen door. Dapika was small, her features slight, fragile, her eyes dark as coal. She opened the screen and her smile, like mine tended to be, was meager and protected, unlike Milo's wide open ones. As usual, I tried to decide if Dapika saw me as a friend or a threat. It was still unclear, though she had little reason to call me friend since I had deemed her a coward. And since I remained uncertain how to remedy that day's outburst, I ignored it.

"I didn't see him, didn't have the chance," I said. "Two girls were running away and begged us to help them escape, so of course Grandmother rushed them back here." I heard the resentment in my voice. "Now I have to start all over again."

Milo cocked his head. "They're here now?"

I picked up a small rock from the ground and threw it. "Yes. Grandmother and Amrita have been talking about it all morning. The girls are from a village near where Grandmother used to live. It's far. Two days by bus. They spent most of last night calling every contact Amrita has but couldn't find out anything about the girls' parents. If they are alive and did escape, they're doing a good job of hiding."

"Maybe they went back to their village," Milo offered.

Dapika sat beside him. "They wouldn't leave their children behind."

I shrugged and threw another rock. "That's the same argument Grandmother and Amrita are having. Grandmother says the safest place for the children would be back in their village, but Amrita says she can't leave her salon for the days it would take to return them, and—"

"And what?" Milo looked at the rock I had picked up and suddenly dropped.

"That's it," I whispered.

"That's what?" Dapika asked. "Why are you whispering?"

I had to get over there right away. "I have to go," I said as I stood. "I'll tell you later." I took off at a run toward Grandmother's house. The moment I opened the door, I called out, "You should take them."

Grandmother looked up from her cup of tea. "Take who?"

"The girls. On the bus. To their village." I bit my lip. My heart raced. She had to agree. This had to work.

"I can't do that." Grandmother shook her head. "I have to stay here with you and help you find your brother."

I had to think quickly. "Well, I've been thinking maybe we shouldn't rush that." Amrita was sitting across from Grandmother, and I felt her eyes on me. "I don't want to mess up by not having thought everything through. What if you went to the village and I went to the House of Hope for the couple of weeks you'd be gone? I could help out on the farm and learn from the rescue team there. Maybe I could develop a better strategy."

Grandmother gazed up at the shelf on the wall, now empty. Before breakfast that morning, I had finally asked her about the idols on her shelf. She had looked aghast and said they were not idols but just figurines. I asked if they were statues of her dead ancestors. Again, she looked horrified at the thought and said no, of course not. Then what were they for? Just decorations, she answered. She then said she had no idea they were a stumbling block. I did not see how one could stumble over them up there on the shelf, but she continued muttering to herself in shocked tones as she took them from the shelf and carried them to her room. "I shall dispose of these immediately," she had said and then talked to herself all the way down the hall. "Imagine, thinking these are idols. How many people have visited my home over the years and thought that same thing? Oh, heavenly Father, I'm so sorry. I never—"

At that point she switched to English, and I missed most of her words. Now as she stared at the blank space, I continued my argument. "You said it takes two days to get there. So if you travel two days there and two days back, you could stay several days to help them get settled again and then go to your old home village for a few days and still be back within two weeks' time." I heard myself babbling, but continued. "I'm sure it's been a long time since you visited your village. You must miss the people there."

"I do." Her voice had gone soft with memories. "It has been many years."

She looked me in the eye. In India we are supposed to look down to show honor, but Grandmother is American and if I looked down, she would think I was hiding something. I did not want her questioning my secrets. So I looked at her face, her nose, as I spoke again. Though I knew it was wrong, I used the final, juiciest piece of bait. "Those girls need your help. Besides, didn't you say that while your protectors were away, you had the chance to have a real adventure?"

Her eyes shone. "You're right. I'll call Asha tonight and arrange for you to stay at the House of Hope." She turned to Amrita. "What do you think?"

Amrita's gaze on me was keen and sharp. Her words came out slow and measured. "Yes, I think Jasmina has come up with a good plan."

Did she guess my secret idea, or was she just referring to the plan about Grandmother and the village? I clasped my hands behind my back and tried to smile like the unselfish person I pretended to be. I hoped Grandmother would not get sick out there so far from a doctor or clinic. My heart hurt imagining how she would feel if she found out what I was planning, when she realized my lie.

I would just have to make sure she did not find out. There was no other choice.

fourteen
The Jesus God

The next day was just what a day should be—bright and sunny. A slight breeze whispered around me as I opened the front door. I was surprised to see Dapika on the porch, sitting with the two young girls from the quarry. She was telling them about the Jesus God and how He loved them.

Had my jaw not been attached, it would have fallen from my face and dropped to the floor. "Dapika? You're a Christian?"

She looked at me, and I was stunned at the peace on her face. "Yes," she said. "I decided to give my life to Jesus that day you stayed home from church."

My eyes went wide. I'd been running around naked and mortifying myself while she was committing her life and her soul for all eternity.

"Who is this Jesus God?" one of the girls asked. "Is He Hindu?"

"No." Dapika hesitated when Amrita approached the house. I wondered if Dapika would stop, but she continued. "Jesus is far above all the gods and goddesses. When I lived with my mother in a terrible, terrible place called a brothel, I watched people come to the Hindu shrines and offer incense and pray for forgiveness."

Amrita crossed her bangled arms. "Before they came in, or after they came out?"

"Both," Dapika answered. She looked back at the children. "Sometimes people prayed for more money to buy drugs. The men and women who bought and sold us prayed for success. The women who were dying prayed for relief from their pain. Everyone wanted something, but no one received peace from that place. No one left with hope."

The children looked up at Dapika as if she had begun to glow. She nearly had. I did not know what to do with myself or with the terrible fear that filled me as she spoke. It propelled me to move, but I did not know if I should move forward toward Dapika's words or away.

"Jesus is the Creator God who made everything. And He is love. He loved us so much, He took the punishment for all we have done wrong. He came to set the captives free, to give liberty. He said He is the Way and the Truth and the Life, and if we believe in Him we get to live forever in a perfect place where there is no more pain or dying, or—"

"Or mean men selling moms and dads and hitting you if you drop rocks?"

Dapika smiled down at the younger girl. "Definitely not that." She looked up at me. "Jasmina, I wish you would believe in Him. He would give you peace." She actually grinned at me. "He has taken my fear away, so you know He must be very powerful."

I backed away. Someone like Dapika needed a Savior, someone to believe in, to lean on. The only person I could depend on was myself. I turned to Amrita. "Are you a follower of Jesus too?"

She shook her head, arms still crossed. "I am not. I know He is true and good, but He asks everything, and I cannot give up the hate in my heart."

That I understood. Just as I could not give up my lie.

"But you should follow Him," Amrita said. I looked at her in surprise, but she was speaking to the children, not me. "Let Him guide you in His good path before you end up on one like mine, full of regret and revenge."

I wanted to ask who was the target of her desired revenge, but Dapika was talking to me about Jesus again. "I don't need a Savior," I interrupted her.

Dapika's voice was soft. "Everyone needs the Savior."

Tears were rushing to flood my eyes. Before I could humiliate myself by crying in front of Amrita, I flippantly replied. "If He's as powerful as you say, let Him come after me then. After all, if He knows everything, He knows where to find me. Right?" I turned and retreated back inside the house. I pushed the door closed and shut my ears to the story Dapika continued outside. If this Jesus knew everything, He knew what I planned to do. I could not ask for His help. I did not need His help.

Yet, if I did not need Him, why did I feel this terrible longing?

Fifteen

Leaving

We stood near the compound gate. Grandmother looked years younger as she said an affectionate goodbye to Milo, Dapika, and the guard. The two girls waited behind her, each clinging to one side of her kameez top.

When she turned to me, I bent low to touch her feet. "Oh, my dear girl," she said, crouching to pull me back up and enfolding me in a hug. The gesture was Western and foreign, but I returned it, wishing I could tell her how grateful I was for her kindness and how sorry I was for what I was about to do. It was not so bad, I told myself. When she got back, if she did find out, she would have to understand. But I knew the Christians thought lying was wrong, and guilt surged through me, knowing she would think less of me if she learned I had used her.

"I talked everything over with Asha last night. We got it all settled before the phone service cut off." She smiled. Technology and third-world countries do not set well with one another sometimes. She put a hand on my shoulder. "Amrita is coming later this afternoon to take you to the House of Hope. Oh, I forgot!" She lifted her one bag and looked around and behind it. "The money for the ride there. Asha left money in a carved box on my dresser. Get enough to pay for both your and Amrita's needs on the journey and enough for the days I am away. There is a phone at the House of Hope. You may try to call me, but I imagine we will have no signal at all in the village."

She hugged me once more. "Thank you, Jasmina," she whispered in my ear. "I never did like the idea of retirement."

I pulled my lips into what I hoped looked like a smile. "Have a wonderful time," I said, waving at the three travelers as they exited the compound gate.

Dapika sighed and turned to me. "I'd ask to go with you to the House of Hope if I weren't needed here to help with the orphan children. It would be nice to see my mother."

Curiosity had me wanting to ask why she lived on the compound if her mother lived at the House of Hope, but fear had me talking in another direction. "That would be nice, but you're right, the kids need you. Two weeks is a long time to be away."

"Yeah." Her shoulders dropped with disappointment. "But maybe I could—"

"Why don't you write her a letter?" I interrupted. "I can take it with me."

"Good idea! I'll do that now."

She headed toward the orphanage building and only Milo was left. His direct gaze had the hair on the back of my neck standing up. "What?"

He looked at me for a moment longer. "I hope you find what you're looking for . . . at the House of Hope."

His voice sounded reproachful or sad. Did he know? I backed away. "I'd—I'd better go pack for the trip."

I turned and headed for Grandmother's home, feeling his eyes follow me. Once inside, I shut the door and leaned against it. The empty shelf on the wall haunted me. I ran to Grandmother's room and hunted for the carved box. Opening it revealed hundreds of rupees. I quickly closed the box and put my head down on the desk. As a street kid, I had stolen and lied and fought. But now I had been given a whole different life. How could I go back to those old ways now that I knew a path that was so much better, so much more beautiful?

I opened and then shut the box again, and pushed it away from me. I turned and searched until I found the quarry map. I would bring it back. I would take nothing.

Quickly, I wrote a small note to Amrita, telling her I had decided to go with Grandmother after all and would be gone for two weeks. Placing it on the dining room table, I took one last look around, pausing at a photo hanging on the wall of Asha, Mr. Mark, and Grandmother, all smiling.

Out the door, halfway across the compound to the gate, Dapika rushed to my side. "Here it is."

I stopped. "Here what is?"

She held out a scrap of paper. "The letter, for my mother."

"Oh, that." I took the paper. "I'll be sure she gets it."

"Where are you going now?"

The guard was opening the gate for me. "I—I—to get snacks for the trip."

"Can I come with you?"

"Oh, well, that would be good." A line of sweat ran down my back. "But—"

A child yelped from the direction of the playground. Dapika winced, and I sighed in relief. "I guess I'd better go help," she said. "I'll see you later."

"See you later," I said. What was one more lie?

sixteen
Returning

By the end of that day, I had returned to the compound twice. The first time occurred less than one minute after I had exited the gate. Fool that I was, I had not thought to get enough money for the rickshaw ride to and from the quarry. Back inside Grandmother's home, I opened the carved box and took only what I would need.

I showed the rickshaw driver the red-marked spot on the map. That man who had chased the girls at the quarry might know where Samir was. Finding him was my first goal.

I fought with my conscience as the rickshaw carried me through the streets of Kolkata, my hands holding Grandmother's money tight in one fist. It was not much, but my mother always told me a thief was a thief whether he stole a diamond or a cucumber. My insides burned, as if I had swallowed the words of the Indian proverb and they proved too spicy a meal for my stomach.

Seeing the quarry again filled me with a mixture of hope and fear.

I took in several deep breaths of clean air as we neared, knowing none could be found once inside. I debated covering myself in quarry dust to appear a quarry slave, but decided my chances of helping Samir get free might be better if I appeared free myself.

I paid the rickshaw driver and asked him to wait. He tilted his head to the side in a yes, and I walked away from the safety of his little pedaled vehicle to the unknown before me. The quarry gate opened, and a massive truck drove through. Luck seemed to be with me. The guard did not see as I slipped in as the truck passed. Few guards were needed, as the children worked mainly in the back of the quarry. Out of sight of the guard, I rose from my crouch and slowly walked down the gravel path packed into a road by the wheels of trucks and cars and the feet of a hundred children.

Around the mounds of stone, those children came into view, some hammering stone into gravel, others carrying the gravel in tin buckets, others returning, pails empty, ready for another load. Memories assaulted me, and I told myself not to cry. I was not here as a slave. I was here to provide freedom for another.

One child, perhaps only five or six, neared me, two buckets hanging from a yoke over his boney shoulders.

"I am looking for the man in charge. Can you help me?" I asked. His eyes lifted to look at me. I had worried about people asking questions, but he did not. He hadn't the energy to be curious. I'd forgotten what that was like. The boy's eyes shifted to a path curving to our left. I thanked him and quickly moved forward before I came up with some ridiculous idea about rescuing him too. Later, once Samir was free, I would tell Amrita about this place. We could then work together and free that little boy.

Someday. But not today.

The path took me toward the shack where we children had piled together at the end of the day too exhausted to do anything but sleep until the morning came. I circled the small building, my steps bringing me back to the door, which suddenly opened and nearly flattened my face. I jumped back. "Hey!"

A hand held the door's edge and then swung the door shut. I found myself facing a boy about sixteen. He might once have been a quarry slave, but no longer. His clothes were old, but free from dust. His hair had no grey coating. Heavy eyebrows knit together when he saw me. "Who are you?" He looked down and then up, eyeing me. "What are you doing here?"

Perhaps I should have coated myself in dust after all, though the sharp, hard look in his eyes made me think that would not have fooled him. Did he remember me from that day when the girls escaped? "I am looking for someone," I said, trying to keep my voice level. I needed to look and sound confident. Older. "I want to know if you have information about a quarry slave named Samir."

He snorted and then blew his nose out onto the ground near his feet. "You've not been here for a while if you think he's still a quarry slave. Why do you want to know about him?"

"He's my brother."

The eyes regarding me flashed a moment and then narrowed again. "You're Jasmina?"

He did know Samir! Hope clouded my judgment. I had lived on the streets long enough to recognize a predator when I encountered one, but months with Asha and Mr. Mark had numbed my senses. I should never have told him anything. Information is power, and I had handed it right over. "Yes, I'm Jasmina. I'm here to help Samir escape."

He laughed, but it was not a happy sound. "He told me about you, but he said you got sold to a brothel owner." His eyes scanned my face, and I shivered. "I can see why."

"I escaped," I said, my voice hard. This conversation was not going as it should. "Where can I find Samir?"

"You want information? Pay for it."

I stepped back. "You can't make me pay to find my own brother."

"Can't I?" He put his face toward mine, and his sneer revealed yellowed teeth. "Information is valuable. For a sister to find her brother, that would be worth a lot."

My teeth clenched. "How much?"

"How much do you have?"

My hand opened to reveal a few coins. "Just enough for a rickshaw ride," I said with satisfaction.

His sneer dropped. "No money, no brother."

"Tell me where to find him." I cursed myself for my naiveté and him for his arrogance.

He crossed his arms. "Bring back five hundred rupees, and I'll take you to Samir myself."

"Five hundred! Where am I supposed to get five hundred rupees? You can buy a baby in the city for not much more than that!"

"But you don't want a baby, do you?" His sneer was back. "Five hundred. I know where he'll be tonight. Bring it by sunset, and before nightfall you'll be with your precious brother again."

seventeen
Sneaking Back

I was walking away when he yelled after me, "Bring extra money with you in case he needs help to buy his freedom."

My feet sped until I was running. "No. No. I won't do it." I fought with myself all the way back to the compound. I paid the rickshaw driver and stood outside the metal gate. "I can't."

Milo's father opened the gate and greeted me. I did not know what to do. When he swung the gate wide, I entered and rounded the path toward Grandmother's house.

"Jasmina!" Dapika came my direction from the playground. "I thought you'd gone already. Amrita was here an hour ago looking for you."

"Oh, uh, she found me." I walked faster, as if I was in a hurry, which I suddenly was. "We started on our way to the House of Hope, but . . ." I gulped. "She, um . . . we forgot the money Asha had left for the trip. She's waiting out in the taxi. I've got to hurry so we can get to the bus station in time."

I grabbed the front doorknob and turned it. Amrita must have locked it after she found my note. "Oh no," I whispered. "What am I going to do now?"

"We can ask one of the other missionaries. I'm sure they'd be happy to loan you the money."

"No!" I said, my words coming out fast. "I don't want to bother them. I'll just—"

I started my way around the house. All the windows were lined with thick bars to keep out thieves like me. There was no way in.

"Didn't Grandmother give you a spare key when you moved in here?" Dapika tried the knob on the back door. "Locked too."

"No, she said she had to keep the spare key where she wouldn't forget it."

Dapika stopped yanking on the doorknob. "And where was that?"

"Oh." Where was my mind? I took a few steps back away from the house to a large bush. I dropped to the ground and swiveled my body until it was under the overhanging leaves. "She must have done this back when the bush was first planted, before it grew half as big as a bed." My fingers dug a small trench around the root base until the edge of a key poked out like the cut-off tail of a gecko. "I got it!"

I backed out from under the bush and held up the rust-covered key. With a wipe from my orna, the caked dirt crumbled from the key and it fit inside the lock. Dapika followed me inside. "Where is the money?"

Money. How I hated it. "In Grandmother's room." I led the way, every step frantically searching for a way out of this tangled web I'd walked into. The carved box was where I'd left it, pushed to the back of the dresser. I opened it.

"You might as well take it all," Dapika said, pulling the pile of bills from the box and handing them to me. "You never know if you'll need extra."

I stood staring at the bills in my hand. No need to count them. Just a glance showed they added up to far more than five hundred rupees.

"You need a bag," Dapika said, rummaging around the room.

My skin was covered in sweat. "I have to go."

She found an over-the-shoulder bag and handed it to me. "You need this. Carrying a wad of money like that is just asking to get robbed."

I choked over words that would not come out.

She looked me over. "Well, didn't you say you were in a hurry?"

"Right." I looked over Grandmother's room. How long would it take before I could come back? Once Samir was free, I would come back and tell Milo and Dapika everything. I would beg Grandmother's forgiveness when she returned, offering myself as a slave for however long it took, until I earned the rupees back.

I handed the key to Dapika. "Would you put this back for me?"

"Sure." She took the key. "Amrita isn't exactly the patient type, not to mention you don't want to miss your bus."

"My bus. Right. I should get stuff for the trip." My conscience went numb, and I scoured the house for other things I might need—food, several bottles of filtered water, and an extra outfit in case there were papers that had to be stamped or signed. That process took a day or two.

With Dapika beside me, I had to keep up the pretense all the way across the compound. She waved at me as I exited, and I was glad to see her face disappear behind the closing gate. I pulled in a deep breath.

In a few short hours, I would find my brother.

Then what?

eighteen
Another Thief

I returned to the quarry at least an hour before sunset. The gate was closed and locked for the night. Unlike the compound gate, this one had steel bars in lines. I looked through the bars and saw a small child squatting near a mountain of stone, twirling his fingers to shape circles in the gravel.

A few taps on the gate got his attention. He stood and ran away.

"No, wait! Come back!"

The boy disappeared around the stone hill. I turned and slumped down, ignoring the dirt as I sat on the ground. What was I going to do now?

"I knew you'd come back."

I jumped up and turned. The boy was there, eyes glittering. "I'm Fayeed, by the way. I made the kid wait to watch for you." His gaze dropped to the bag draped over my shoulder, clutched in both my hands. "You brought the money?"

My fingers tightened, and I nodded. He pushed a hand through the bars. "Give it to me."

"Take me to my brother first."

"Not a chance." He spread his fingers and held his open palm toward me. "The money first."

What else could I do? I reached into the bag and with my fingers counted the right number of bills. Fayeed's eyes on me made me clumsy. I dropped the bills twice and had to start over.

When I pulled out the correct amount and handed it over, Fayeed's fingers curled around the money as he pulled his hand back inside the gate. He stuffed the bills into his pants pocket and then pulled out a key and unlocked the padlock securing the gate. I expected him to come out, but instead he motioned me in.

"Aren't you taking me to find Samir?"

"I said I would. Come in."

Everything about him was suspicious, like a coiled snake that looks relaxed but in truth might be tensed and ready to strike. My need to find Samir forced me to act according to a trust I did not feel. I entered the quarry and clutched my bag against me when I heard his key securing the padlocked chain around the gate again. Why was he locking it if we would be leaving soon?

"Follow me."

He led me down the path to the back of the quarry. Children were coming in from the mounds. Only the youngest showed interest as they came near and joined our walk, bringing clouds of dust with them. They seemed fascinated with my clean clothing and skin. One young girl started to ask me a question but was cuffed by Fayeed. I sucked in a breath. She immediately went silent, holding a hand to her temple as we walked the rest of the way to the small shack. I shuddered at my memories of those wood slat walls and tin roof, the hard floor inside with no mats where we dropped with exhaustion each night.

I told Fayeed I would wait outside while he got whatever papers he needed. "Go inside," he ordered. The children filed in, eyes down at their feet. He continued to hold the door open. "You too."

I shook my head. "Our agreement was that you would take me to Samir. Tonight."

"I lied." He shrugged, no remorse in his eyes or posture. "You will see your brother, but not tonight. He is coming here tomorrow. Stay here and you will not need to find him, for he will find you."

Could I believe him? Of course not. He said himself he lied.

It was too late to back out now. I had Asha's money in Grandmother's bag. Anger shot from my eyes toward Fayeed, but he seemed to enjoy seeing it, so I put my eyes down and followed the line of children until I, too, was inside.

My body had become used to the comfort of a soft bed, privacy, and space to move. None of those were available that night in the quarry shack. Arms and legs of children draped over me. One child rolled over in the night, his arm flinging over and smacking me in the face. I lay staring at the tin roof, wondering if Samir really was coming to the quarry in the morning, or if that was another lie. Fayeed could keep asking for payment, and I would have to give it to him. How much would he want before it was enough?

By morning such fears were needless, not because things got better, but because they got worse.

I woke at dawn to find my bag empty and all the money gone.

nineteen
Owned Again

"You took my money!"

"Of course I did. Five hundred rupees to let you know your brother was coming right back here to this spot." He sneered at me, and I felt ready to burst from anger.

"There were thousands of rupees in here." I held the bag open, showing it empty. "You stole them while I slept." I never should have closed my eyes.

His sneer spread. "Oh, that's too bad. One of the kids must have taken it. Just think how many coconut-milk popsicles that much money can buy."

"*You* took it." I thrust my hand out toward him, desperation turning my words into a hiss. "Give it back. Now."

"You forget where you are and who is in charge." The reminder was hard and cold like his eyes. My own filled with tears. All hopes of returning to Asha and Grandmother became as empty as the bag I held. They would not want me to hate, but I did. I hated him so much my body shook with it. He pulled a set of keys from one of his pants pockets and a cell phone from the other. I had not noticed the car waiting at the gate, but at the sight of the keys in Fayeed's hand, fear wrapped around the hate in my heart and clenched tight. My breath came in heaving gasps but stopped completely when the car pulled up beside me and the passenger window lowered.

A face appeared, smiling and smooth. "Hello, beautiful," the quarry owner said. I did not have to see his fancy clothes or his shiny shoes. This man was no stranger. I saw his face in my nightmares, focused on me as it was right then. "You look familiar."

The man's gaze drifted lazily to Fayeed. "Is this one of ours?"

This. As if I were a plastic trinket in a roadside stall. *I am a person!* I wanted to scream. *I do not belong here.*

Fayeed shot a look my way, eyebrows up, and I saw myself as helpless as he knew me to be. One word and this man would own me again. Fayeed had the keys, the money, and the knowledge. I had no defense.

Silently, my eyes pleaded with him. He gave a slight nod, then turned to the man in the car. "No," Fayeed said. "She's . . ."

I held my breath again.

"She's . . . a friend . . . of Samir's. Says she has a message for him from his sister."

Breath escaped my burning lungs. The quarry owner looked me over. "A shame," he said. "Pretty girls are always welcome."

My face burned along with my lungs as the car pulled away, leaving Fayeed and me in a cloud of quarry dust, as if the man purposefully coated us in a grey reminder of his power and position. I coughed and Fayeed wiped impatient hands down his shirt. The phone in his hands beeped twice, and he flipped it open and pushed a button. I watched and waited until he closed the phone and looked at me.

"That was a text from Samir," he said, and I felt my heart speed up.

"Is he coming?"

"He wants me to bring you to him."

I still clutched the empty bag in my hands, foolishly clinging to the memory of what once filled it. "You said he would come here."

Fayeed shrugged. "He doesn't want to. We'll get an auto, and I'll take you to him."

I did not trust him, but what could I do? I saw victory in Fayeed's eyes, and in that look I felt the bars lower and cage me in. He had not handed me over to the quarry owner because he wanted to own me himself. My only hope was finding Samir and convincing him to escape with me.

"Let's go then," I said, hoping our ride would take me deeper into the city and not deeper into Fayeed's control.

twenty
Found

As we rode away from the quarry, my subtle attempts to memorize turns and street names did not go unnoticed. Fayeed ordered the driver to stop. He yanked my orna from my shoulder and, while I protested, twisted the cloth and then wrapped it around my face in a blindfold. "Some things are best kept secret," he whispered near my ear. I wanted to elbow him away from me. His breath on my neck was worse than the summer heat.

Fayeed gave a command to the driver, and we moved forward. Unable to see anything, I strained my ears for sounds that would help me discern our location or at least which part of the city we were in. Each time my body swayed as the auto swerved right or left, I marked it in my mind, but after twelve turns I lost count. Were we really traveling that far, or was he merely having the driver circle the same block or two to confuse me?

When we stopped, I tried to sift through the sounds assaulting us. A fruit seller called out as he passed by. Many horns indicated a busy road. The discordant caws of a crow joined music blaring from several directions. A woman's voice yelled about someone not paying her full price for a basket of dried fish. Ah, so that was the smell.

A hand touched my head, and I jerked away.

"If you want this blindfold off, be still."

Fayeed sat very close. I turned my head so he could untie my orna and turned my body away from him. The cloth fell away, and I shielded my eyes from the light, taking in the scene around me.

My weeks living on the street before I met Asha had not brought me to this area. Even had I approached, I would have turned away. How had Samir come to be in a place such as this? Broken glass bottles made an unpleasant mosaic across the sidewalk near my feet. I carefully stepped down, knowing my sandaled feet would not fare well against a chunk of sharp glass. I stood facing a long concrete wall mottled over with faded posters of long-forgotten movies, rain and time having shredded them into strips of false promises. A crowd of men sat in a circle on the sidewalk to my left, ignoring irritated pedestrians as they gambled and laughed. A child ran by, his leg clipping the back of one of the men. The next instant, the child was on the pavement, crying, while the man who had reached back to trip him cursed at him for messing up his turn with the dice.

A part of me wanted to go to the child's aid, if not to help, at least to comfort, but I wanted to get wherever we were going, get my brother, and leave this place as soon as possible. Something I could not define filled the air with evil. Maybe the area was cursed. A sickly smell, different than the rank smell of the dried fish stall near the road, followed us and grew stronger as Fayeed led me down the sidewalk to a narrow passageway between two buildings. Despite my careful steps, I could not avoid the water that had collected into small pools along our path. My feet and ankles were wet and dirty by the time we emerged into a wider alleyway between two buildings. A rat scurried near my feet, and I screamed.

"You shouldn't fear the rats here," Fayeed said, obviously amused. "There are much bigger rats where we are headed."

I followed him up a metal staircase once painted green but now covered more in rust than paint. The steps screeched under his weight. Was he talking about rats like the one I had just seen or the human kind?

We climbed on, the flights of stairs forming Z shapes up the outer wall of the building. I cinched my orna around my waist to keep it from touching the mold thriving along the walls. Ropes hung from the windows of the nearest building across the alley to the other; wet saris and lungis dripped onto me from above. A bright orange sari hung over the third-floor stairs. Fayeed pushed it out of the way. It slipped from the rope, and I tried to catch it, but the material drifted out of reach. Fayeed did not even turn to see it land in the mud-crusted puddles on the ground.

"Come on," he said gruffly, stopping on the fourth-floor landing and inserting a key into a lock. How many keys did he oversee? Fayeed pushed several times on the stubborn door. It would not give way until he gave it a hard, swift kick. "Welcome to the palace." He ushered me in with a bow that was far from sincere.

I passed him and stepped inside. Dank, humid air clouded the room, sticking to my skin and hair. As my eyes adjusted to the lack of light, I realized the room was not empty, as I had first assumed. A man sat in the far corner, cigarette in hand, smoke billowing around him. His eyes were unfocused and glazed over. He did not acknowledge our presence or even seem to know we were there.

The smell was worse in the room than it had been outside. My stomach lurched. I found my way to a doorway with a curtain draped from a rope strung across its frame. Pushing it aside, I cautiously peered into another room, dirtier than the first. Tin plates with leftover rice lay piled in a heap on the floor, while several rats enjoyed the feast.

"Are those the rats you were talking about?" I asked, gagging.

Fayeed's voice was at the back of my neck. "Oh, no. We're looking for bigger ones."

He put a hand to my back, and I moved forward, more in complaint of the inappropriate touch than my desire to see any more. Another doorway across the room lay bare and uncurtained. I stepped into the third room and bit my lip.

Three young men sat counting piles of rupee bills. The two facing the door were unknown to me, but the third was not. Even from the back I knew him.

I had found my brother.

twenty-one
A Fool

"Samir."

His head whipped around, and suddenly he stood in front of me. He looked like an actor practicing facial expressions; his eyes went wide in surprise, his lips curved as if he might be glad to see me, and then his eyebrows narrowed with questions.

I fought tears. After all these months, all my fears that he'd been sold to another country or hurt. Now here he was. For a moment I forgot the stolen money and my desperate circumstances and allowed my heart to feel a trickle of hope.

Samir took a step toward me. His eyes might have lit up, but then he saw Fayeed behind me and his face changed. "Who are you?" he said.

I looked back at Fayeed and then at Samir, but Samir wasn't looking at Fayeed. He was asking me. I gaped at him, but Fayeed laughed. "Here's your sister, Samir. She's been searching for you. Had a nice wad of money on her." I stared as Samir's face closed hard as granite stone and Fayeed's voice dropped. "You've been holding out on me."

The sinister edge to his tone was not missed by me or Samir. My brother looked at me. "You're a fool," he said.

A fool. All those months worrying about him. Searching for him. All I had sacrificed to find him, and that is all he had to say to me? In my imagination I kicked him in the shin like I used to when we were children. In real life I sniffed. When I saw his shoulders tense up and remembered how he hated that, I sniffed again.

Fayeed had nudged around me and the door's small opening and spoke quietly to Samir. I watched Samir shake his head, glare at Fayeed, and then pick up one of the large stacks of bills and place it in Fayeed's outstretched hand. Fayeed unbuttoned the top two buttons of his shirt and put the money in a hidden pocket inside. He whispered something to Samir, and Samir responded with words I could not hear, though I recognized in the low growl a threat.

I turned and flattened my back against the wall when Fayeed passed me on his way out. "So glad I could help you find your precious brother," he said, stopping in front of me and bending to put his face near mine. "Now that you have no money . . ." He smiled and I shrank away from his hot breath on my face. "Come and find me if you need a job. I'd take good care of you." He chuckled and pulled out his cell phone. Rather than holding it to his ear, he held it out between us in front of me. I heard a click, and then after pushing a button, he turned the phone around and on the screen I saw myself. His phone had taken a photograph of me. How was that possible?

Before I could ask him why he had taken my picture or ask him to destroy it, he was gone. Samir gave a command, and the two other boys rose and followed him. My brother, who was no longer little, stacked the remaining piles of money and stuffed them into a zippered pouch. He stood and faced me. I could see the boy I used to know in the near man now regarding me with disdain.

"What did he mean about a job?" I asked, not knowing what else to say. Any hopes I might have had of a joyful reunion or gratitude or even welcome had exited right before Fayeed had.

Samir ignored my question. "You were sold from the quarry months ago. Where did they take you, and how did you manage to come here with the money Fayeed said you had?" His jaw set. "Or did someone send you?"

Somewhere between my money being stolen and my brother calling me a fool, my old street smarts rose to the surface. My instincts told me Samir was no victim in need of rescue, and though I could not determine why, I knew I could not trust him with honest information. "No one sent me. I escaped and have been living on the streets," I said. There was no need to tell him about Asha and Mark or about the rescues.

He scrunched up his face like he always did when he did not believe me and stepped closer. "Where did you get the money?"

My hands gripped Grandmother's bag.

"You might as well tell me." Samir knelt in front of a large black box. He turned a knob in one direction, then another, several times until I heard a click from the inside. The front part of the box swung open, like Grandmother's refrigerator, and Samir tossed the zippered pouch inside. "Fayeed said you had money. From the look on his face I can guess you don't have it anymore. You couldn't have managed to live on the streets but still be stupid enough to walk into Fayeed's traps. You've been someplace or have some rich friends."

I shuddered, but outwardly remained calm. "I stole the money," I said. It was ironic that I cared enough to tell myself that was not an outright lie, since I had actually stolen. "From a rich American who wasn't paying attention." That was true also. Grandmother was rich, and she wasn't paying attention when I took the money from the box. She was a hundred kilometers away, thinking I was spending two weeks at the House of Hope, never imagining I'd be in a place like this.

"And you've been on the streets with a bunch of money all these weeks." Doubt filled his words.

"Of course not," I argued. "I just got the money yesterday."

"And you came to the quarry right after?"

I nodded. "I stole it to buy your freedom."

Samir closed the door to the box and then reached into a cardboard container near it and pulled out a bottle. I knew what beer bottles looked like, having seen many littering the roads, but could not hide my surprise that my brother, only thirteen, was drinking one. I must admit my first thought was not how it might harm him, but how much it must cost.

"I am free," he said, taking a long swig from the bottle. "No more slaving away my life for idiots like the quarry boss or the garment factory boss. I'm the boss now. I make the rules, and I make the money."

The room seemed to fill with bright possibilities. "If you have money," I said. "Then we can use it to find our parents."

He swallowed more beer, then belched loudly. "Why would I want to do that?"

twenty-two
My Parents

I turned away from the complete lack of interest in Samir's eyes. "I've been searching for you, trying to find some way to set you free or help you escape, so we could find our parents and be a family again."

He scoffed in response, as if I had told a joke that was not funny. "The parents who sold us? They're the reason we became slaves. Have you forgotten the three years in the garment factory?"

"No," I whispered. Memories still woke me in the night. "I haven't forgotten, but maybe Father is sorry now that he sold us. Maybe he wants us back and has been looking for us."

Samir scoffed again, a mixture of anger and disgust. "You know nothing. They never looked for us. Father got rid of us on purpose, so he could get a job." He drained the bottle. "They got what they deserved."

"What do you mean? What has happened to them?"

He tossed the bottle onto the pile of used dishes in the middle of the room. Tin plates crashed, and rice flew. "I know what happened, and I'm glad it happened. They're the slaves now, and I'm the one who is free."

"Samir—"

He pulled the curtain aside and stepped into the first room. "I have to get you out of here and find someplace for you to stay. You were stupid enough to tell Fayeed you're my sister, so he'll plan to use that against me if he can."

I followed him, asking questions. He told me to keep my mouth shut and he'd tell me on the way.

"On the way" must have meant once we were in a rickshaw because Samir was silent down the four flights of stairs, across the muddied pathway, and onto the sidewalk. I clamped my lips between my teeth to keep the questions inside through long, torturous minutes until we were finally on the road.

"Please tell me about our parents," I begged. "Asha took me back to the ocean, and the house was gone. It got swept out to sea in a cyclone, and nobody knew if they were even alive, and—"

"Who is Asha?"

Samir's eyes were on me, and I could have kicked myself. When would I learn to think before letting words fly out of my mouth? "Tell me about our parents first," I said, looking away so he could not see through me and know I would be searching my imagination for a credible story to tell him. We passed several roads and alleys. One looked familiar, but I could not recall why.

He told the rickshaw driver to stop and talked as he paid him. "Our parents are in a rich neighborhood on the other side of the city."

"Rich? I thought you said they were slaves."

"You really don't get any of this, do you?" he asked, his tone letting me know those months of separation had not changed his general contempt for me. I wanted to kick myself again— no, I wanted to kick him. Why couldn't he be like Milo?

He led me toward a building with a modeling agency sign hanging above the door, but then steered me away and down alongside the building until we turned the corner and stood near the blank sidewall. "Listen well, because I'm only saying this once. Remember the day of the fire in the garment factory?"

I nodded. I could still see the flames coming toward us and feel the heat against my face.

"That morning I had annoyed the boss. I don't remember why, but he took the whip from the overseer and was whipping me himself. While he did, he told me his usual speech about how he owned us all and we would never get away. He wanted me to cry out, to beg for mercy, and when I didn't, he got angry and started telling me that I was there because my father loved money more than me."

A huge bus lumbered past on the road parallel to where we stood, its horn blast deafening. I held my ears and yelled, "You already knew that."

He bent his head to the left in agreement and spoke normally once the bus was gone. "That's what I said, but he said I didn't know anything. He started bragging about how he got entire families to be his slaves. He would send a man to villages like ours, where he would offer jobs in rich homes for men to work the landscape or be guards and women to clean or cook. Of course he promised them high pay and wonderful lives."

I swatted at a mosquito. "What does that have to do with us?"

Samir swatted at me. "Be quiet and let me finish." I stared at the top button on his shirt and kept my mouth closed.

"The catch was that these rich people didn't want children, so you could only get the job if you didn't have any kids with you." A silence filled the space between us as he waited for me to . . . what? Figure out that—that—

"That's why he sold us both away." I felt like I had just swallowed a big rock, and it lay heavy in my stomach.

Samir's eyes did not reflect the pain that filled mine. They were full of anger. "The boss let them think about his offer, then returned to our house the following week and offered his lies, knowing the trap was set. Father took the bait and the money. He sold us away so he could get a great job, but the boss was lying about the job just as he lied about our free education."

"What happened to them?"

His jaw worked, and he put a fist against the wall and leaned on it. "They left home and went to their new jobs in some rich person's house. They are still there, not making any money, working from sunrise till sunset, living in a basement. They're slaves, and I hope they are as miserable as they made us."

I stepped away from this boy who talked like a man full of hate. "How can you say that? They are our parents."

The eyes looking into mine were black as night. "I want them to suffer," he said. "I want all of them to suffer. The garment factory boss, the quarry boss, all of them will pay for what they did to us." His fist punched the wall. "Especially Gar, the garment factory owner. He already paid some, but he will pay more."

My mind reeled, but I caught the satisfaction in his voice. "What do you mean, he's already paid some? Samir, what have you done?"

He gave me a terrible smile. "That fire that destroyed his factory? I started it."

twenty-three
Revenge

My ears heard the words, but my mind could not believe them. Our parents, slaves? The garment factory boss, planning to trap and traffic us all from the beginning? Samir setting a fire that destroyed an entire building? "We could have all died." My voice was hoarse. I looked up at him, only then realizing he had grown taller than me. "How could you do it?"

His shrug seemed casual, but the glint in his eyes was hard. "Without a whip in his hand, Gar is just a fat coward. I knew he'd open the door to save himself."

I slid down to the sidewalk, my legs unable to support me. "But why?" I'm not certain what I was even asking. *Why did the garment factory owner connive to take us all? Why did my father believe him? Why had my brother risked hundreds of children's lives?*

Samir squatted down beside me. My eyes were on my hands, palms open in my lap, as if holding them out waiting to be handed an answer I could wrap my fingers around and keep.

"He paid me to do it," Samir whispered.

I looked up at his face, the boyish cheeks now long and angular. "Who?"

"He said he'd give me a high position. I'd never be a slave again." My brother stood and kicked the hard wall behind us. "He was right about that."

My feet tingled and burned as I stood to face him. "Who?" I asked again. He couldn't mean the garment factory owner, but who else did Samir know except the other children on the streets? None of them could promise freedom.

Samir kicked the wall again, his rage frightening me. "I've already told you too much. You're obviously not smart enough to keep your mouth shut about anything."

Tears burned the back of my eyes, but he ignored them, piercing me with a glare. "Come with me." He yanked my arm, and I had no option but to accompany him.

He dragged me back toward the main door of the building under the modeling sign. Letters boasted, "We give you your dreams," next to a picture of a beautiful girl with luxurious thick hair and full lips stuck out in a pout.

"What does that sign say?" I knew what it said, of course, but was stalling for time before we went inside. The darkened windows across the front made me uneasy.

The hand not gripping my arm hauled back and slapped me across the face. I stared in shock. Who had my brother become? I let the tears spill out, hoping they would shame him.

He pulled me to face him, his head higher than mine now. "Don't ever, *ever* remind me you can read and I can't." He called me a foul name, and I cringed. As awful as he had been as a child, it had been an annoying awful, not this fearful evil I saw in him now.

"What has happened to you, Samir?" I whispered, another tear rolling down my cheek.

Gruffly he released me with a shove. "Tell me who Asha is and where you really got that money," he ordered.

"I—I—when I escaped, they chased me. I tried to outrun them, but ended up in an alley with no way out. I yelled for help, and this woman opened a door and pulled me in just in time. She let me take a bath and gave me clean clothes. She was . . . kind." It was an easy story to tell, my memories making my voice soft and sincere. I wished I could find that woman again and thank her. At the time, I feared she was a trafficker too, and I had run away. "She said she would take me to a Christian orphanage."

Samir scoffed. "Christians. They pay money to buy converts. They want to convert all of India and take it over to make it Western." He opened the door to the building and pushed me inside.

"No, they don't," I said. "They care about people and help people. They showed more love to me than my family ever did." A little burned pride crept into my voice, a little hurt. Once again I had let my feelings guide my words and tangle my story.

"They? I thought you said it was one woman." Samir guided me through a main waiting area filled with empty chairs and then down a hallway with several closed doors.

I stopped wondering what was behind the doors and concentrated on building a solid lie. "Well, she took me to the orphanage, and . . . I stayed there for a while." I shrugged. "They gave me free food and a place to sleep. It was better than the streets."

"And their free food convinced you to reject the religion of your ancestors and be a Christian?"

"No. Don't be ridiculous." We walked all the way to the end of the hallway. Samir stood facing the back wall, like a man without sense. "What are you doing?"

"Shut up," he ordered. "So how did you end up back on the streets, and how did you get the money?"

I wanted to point out that he had given me opposing commands, but had no desire to get slapped again. He knocked on the wall, and the wall slid away. I stared at a set of stairs leading down to a hidden . . . something. "Go," he said, and I obeyed. I began answering his questions, for some reason now whispering as we descended into the dark.

"After a few weeks, I ran away. I wanted to come find you, but I knew if you were still trapped at the quarry, I'd need money to get you out. So I sneaked back into the orphanage one night and stole the money the woman had just gotten from sponsors." My lie got bigger, but it sounded convincing, at least to me. "She trusted me and had shown me where she kept it."

"Why would she trust you?" We were in some kind of underground room. In the uneven light of one exposed light bulb surrounded by moths, Samir looked me over. "I guess you do look like someone who can be trusted by naive, good people."

Was that a compliment or an insult? I asked my own question, hoping to distract him from finding any holes in my lie. "Who paid you to start the fire in the garment factory?"

"I never said he paid me." I watched a fearsome smile cross his face. "He never planned to pay me, but I made sure he did. I'm not finished with him either. They will both answer to me one day. I will rule this kingdom, and they will serve me."

Had my brother gone insane? What was he talking about?

twenty-four
Merchandise

"You will stay here."

I stopped questioning my brother's sanity, certain now he was crazy. "I will not." He reached his hand back. "Don't you dare strike me again," I said, my voice fierce enough that he dropped his hand and looked at me with a speck of respect. "I will not stay in this—this hovel. It's rank and damp and dark. I will live on the streets before I stay in a place like this."

"You may have to," he said, pulling the dingy cord hanging from the light and leaving us in darkness except for the shaft of light coming from the top of the stairs. He led the way back up. "If you hadn't been stupid enough to give Fayeed all your money, we wouldn't be in this mess."

"I didn't give him all my money. He stole it!"

Samir sighed the way he used to when I would not do his chores for him. We reached the top of the stairs, and I was glad when he slid the wall section closed. "Wait." I reached out and touched it. "You knocked and this opened by itself?"

He pushed my hand away and clicked the section into place. "If you'd actually been living on the streets like you said, you should be more observant. There are two girls hiding down there. There's a button they can push from the bottom of the stairs to open the door when someone knocks."

My jaw dropped. "In that place? What for? And why didn't they say anything?"

"They are there because—it doesn't matter why. They have learned to keep quiet. Unlike you."

How many times that day had I thought about kicking him? "If they can open the door, why do they not just leave that terrible place?"

"You ask too many questions." Samir opened the second door we came to on the left in the hallway. "Will you be more comfortable in here, Princess?" His voice dripped with sarcasm. I took in the small room stocked with cameras and other equipment I did not recognize. A square object sitting on a desk I knew to be a computer. Asha and Mr. Mark had one. I had never used it myself, but I had seen them moving a small oval-shaped device that made clicking sounds and seemed to make the box change. Sometimes the box even made noise and showed pictures like a television.

Two rolled-up mats leaned against the wall. There was enough bare floor space to spread them out with a little room to spare. "Why can't I just stay with you?" I had no idea where he lived, but with all these connections he was unlikely to still be on the streets.

"Where I live the men like girls like you."

"Then that would be good. They would help protect me."

His look sent shivers down my spine. "They are the kind of men you need protection from, big sister." He shook his head. "You really are naive, aren't you?"

"Well, if I'm so naive, why don't you tell me what's going on so I won't be anymore?"

By the end of my sentence, I was shouting. The next thing I knew, Samir had his hand over my mouth and was backing me against the wall. "You want everyone to know that you're ignorant and can be used?" His voice lowered, and I watched his mouth move over words that only added to my confusion. "Gar owns this place. After the garment factory was destroyed, he found an easier way to make money. He targets girls just like you, young and exploitable. So does the quarry owner and any other man or woman in my business who has the chance."

I pulled his hand from my face and whispered, "If they are all so bad, why do you work with them?"

He sighed again, leaning his hand against the wall above my head. "You would never understand. This is who I am now, and there's no going back." He looked at me and for a moment I thought I saw a flicker of caring in his gaze. "You can stay here for now since there's no way you can go back to that orphanage now that you stole their money, but you have to do as I say. If you don't, and they get you, I'm not going to sacrifice all I've worked for to save you."

He was right. I did not understand any of this. "I sacrificed everything to come save you."

"And look how that turned out."

The tears were back. "I want to see our mother, Samir. I want to go home."

He turned away from me. "There is no home, Jasmina. No family. We're not wanted, just like all the other kids on this street."

"Maybe Father felt that way, but Mother didn't. You know she didn't. How can you let her suffer?"

"She let me suffer, didn't she? She didn't stop him." He looked at me. "You didn't either. Why didn't any of us fight, Jasmina? Why did we all just let it happen?"

A door shut somewhere nearby. Samir rushed to the open doorway and looked down the hall. He greeted someone, and a man's voice responded. The sound brought up memories of foot-pedal sewing machines and long days bent over foreign clothing.

In panic I looked around the room for a place to hide, or better yet a window to climb out of and escape. The room had no window, and even the largest pieces of equipment in the room were items on long poles, nothing wide enough to conceal my red outfit. I ran to the wall nearest the door and pushed myself as far into the corner behind Samir and the door as possible.

twenty-five
The Boss

The effort was futile. The man squeezed his massive body through the small doorway, and in three seconds had his eyes on me.

I am sure it was clear that I was terrified. Standing before me, much too close, was the man of my nightmares. The man who'd kept me in a closed brick building for three years, never once giving me even ten minutes to breathe fresh air or enjoy a moment's sunlight.

"Well, now, who is this delightful creature?"

I trembled head to foot. Samir looked at me and shrugged. "She's nobody. I hired her to help me do a job."

My breathing came in short puffs as he grinned at me. Now I understood what Fayeed meant about the rats. They were the human kind.

My hands clung to Grandmother's bag hanging at my hip, a useless gesture as it certainly was little barrier, as he stepped closer and lifted his hand. "You look familiar." He touched my hair, and I pulled away, looking to Samir for help. He glanced at Samir as well. "Is she related to you? A cousin perhaps?"

Had Fayeed told him who I was, and he was testing us, or did he really not recognize me? Samir's hands clenched at his sides, but his voice remained casual. "I don't have any cousins that I know of. She's just some girl I found, a runaway. Maybe when I'm finished with her, she'll want to work for you."

I swallowed my horror, not so ignorant that I did not recognize the plea in Samir's eyes that I play along. I gave the maggot of a man a tremulous smile, my eyes focused on his chin as I could not get myself to look him full in the face. I did not speak, for if he truly did not recognize me, my voice might be familiar enough to give me away.

"A delightful prospect," he murmured, putting a finger under my chin and turning my face to the right and left. He looked back at Samir. "Let's keep your little friend our secret, shall we? We don't need to tell my partner she's here."

He swept his hand around the room and gave a bow, a small one since his middle gave little room for bending. "You are welcome here, young lady. Stay as long as Samir needs you. After that . . ." He shifted his weight from one foot to the other, and I imagined him a king cobra swaying before the strike. "We can discuss your future possibilities with us."

Would he leave now? My hands ached from holding the bag so tightly. He turned and on his way out put a hand on Samir's shoulder. "Nice work, son," he said. Samir flinched at the title and shut the door behind him.

"I don't think he knows who you are," he said, looking over at me. "He remembers pretty girls and forgets everyone else, and you have changed." His gaze then traveled over the room. "Stay here until we decide what job you should do to earn your keep and pay for your food. Do not leave this room without me, and whatever you do, do not do anything Fayeed says. He is the only person who knows who you are; stay away from him. He's a thief and a liar and can't be trusted."

As you are, I thought. My chin went high until I realized those words now described me as well.

"Right now I can't think of anything you can do that won't cause me trouble. You talk too much and don't have the good sense to know a jackal from an alligator. I wish I could send you to our parents and be done with it."

"I wish you would." Was he waiting for me to thank him? I stepped across the room and pulled one mat from the wall. "Go away," I said, my back to him.

The door slammed, and I turned to see that he had left without saying a word. I dropped to the floor in silence, the mat falling beside me, and waited until I was sure he would not return before I allowed myself to cry.

twenty-six
Lost

Dear Mother,

In the city during monsoon season the water fills the open sewers that border the roads. If the rains do not stop, the sewers overflow, and the streets flood. It is terrible living in Kolkata at such times, awash with a layer of waste.

I am Kolkata in monsoon season. Shame, once kept contained, now floods everything I say and do. I am a thief, a liar, betrayer of those most kind to me. Once I hoped I could do enough good, rescue enough victims, to have my sins forgiven. Now I know I am unforgivable. Even if I stretched out penance or payment among all the gods, it could never erase what I have done. My only hope, my only chance, is to survive this operation tomorrow. If I do, I can pay back what I took and then come find you and free you. If not, Samir will take the money gained by the loss of my life, and no one will ever know how much I risked to set things right.

You must tell them, Mother. If I die and Samir brings this notebook to you, you must get to Asha and Grandmother and tell them everything. Samir will not offer freedom to you; you must take it. Tell him you know about the money from my kidney. Tell him I died for that money, and he must use it to set you free. He will keep the rest, but please, I beg you, go to the missionary compound near the second largest banyan tree (taxi drivers will know where it is) and find Asha. By the time you are free, she will have returned. She will wonder why I left and will want to search for me. You must stop her from entering this world of death and darkness. And when you tell her about the money, tell her I'm sorry; I tried to repay her.

This night is nearly half over, my nightmare ready to begin with the day. The girl in my room cries even in her sleep. My own tears drop to mar the pages as I write.

Grandmother once told me that heaven is not a place where gods and goddesses cheat and betray, love and hate, and play with us mortals and our pain. She said it is a pure place with no sorrow or pain and no more death. It is light, but not from the sun. God is the light, and He cannot have any darkness in His heaven.

If it is true that God cannot be where darkness thrives, then He is far from this place.

I want to stop writing, to end this story before further expressing the shame of those days. I want to burn this notebook and erase my words, to never have you know what I have become. Only my fear of death keeps my pen moving. Each time I stop, the thought of what will happen to me when I die is a terror I cannot bear. A poster on the concrete wall next to me shows a Hindu god and goddess together in a way that cannot be called holy. They do not care what will happen to me. No matter how many marigold garlands get draped over their framed painting, they cannot help.

No one can help me. I am lost.

twenty-seven
Snakes and Charmers

No exaggeration coats my words when I say the next two days were miserable. Samir treated me like the dirt beneath his feet. Gar, the garment factory owner, kept finding reasons to come to my room, every time looking at me in a way I did not understand but definitely did not like. I did not fear for my life, but I did fear the day that Gar would want take me away and I would refuse and end up in that moldy basement with no light and no hope.

From waking to sleeping, every day I had more questions, but no one to answer them. Samir told me nothing. He only came when he had papers he wanted me to read to him. Sometimes he told me to find something on the computer for him and explain it. Other times he dictated messages and had me type them onto the screen in a way to send words without paper called e-mails. I asked him how such a marvel worked, and he told me to shut up and be useful.

"Our mother would be ashamed of you," I said and got a smack on the back of my head in reply.

One advantage of Samir thinking I was stupid was that he did not bother to hide his conversations from me, assuming I could not comprehend them. I listened and gathered bits and pieces of information like broken seashells on the beach. At night alone in my room in that strange, mysterious building, I worked to assemble the pieces. I discovered the quarry owner had partnered with the garment factory owner not long after the fire. I had yet to figure out why. Gar had nothing but a burned-out building. All the children had fled. Why would the quarry owner accept him as a full partner if he had nothing to offer? Or was it a case of blackmail, which seemed to be the power behind almost all the decisions made in this area?

After days trapped in the camera room, Samir decided I would not ruin his life by emerging, so he started sending me on errands. The first time, he came with me, showing me where to buy certain things, which sections of the area to avoid, and who was not to be trusted, which was nearly everyone. On one street, I noticed a crowd gathering. "What is happening?"

"Who knows?" Samir said. "Probably a fight. Let's go."

I ignored him. We were no longer children, and I was not going to let him boss me around every minute. I tried to politely find a way through the crowd, but when that failed, I pushed my way in. Samir followed and grabbed my arm. "Come on."

My eyes did not leave the scene before me. "No. It's a snake charmer. I've never seen one before." I watched in sick fascination as the man, naked from the waist up, a turban wrapped around his small head, opened a large wicker basket while playing an Asian melody on a bamboo flute. He had squatted in front of the basket, and his right knee swayed back and forth. A cobra rose slowly from the basket, its flared head swaying in mirror image of the man's knee movements.

"Snakes are deaf, you know," Samir said behind me. "It's all a show, them dancing to the music. They're just following the motions he's making. Even the snake charmers are liars."

We were mashed in the crowd, and I knew he would not hit me in front of all these people, so I kicked my foot backward until it encountered his shin. Did he have to ruin everything?

He pinched my arm from behind, and I elbowed him. "Do you realize you lock me away just like the garment factory owner did? You're no better than he is." I made my words as angry as I could. It was better than crying.

No response came from behind me, and I wondered if he had left me. It would be my good fortune if he had, I told myself. With stubborn resolve, I did not look back to see if he was still there, keeping my eyes on the snake charmer and his three snakes. The man pulled the first snake from the largest basket, extending it from its coil. It stretched longer than the man's height. I clapped with the others as he put the snakes each in their own basket and closed the lids over them. Coins were dropped into a tin cup near the man's feet. I had none to give and began backing away when Samir finally spoke. "Stay and watch," he said.

Curious, I stood still and waited. The crowd dispersed, and the man hung his baskets onto a yoke he lifted onto his shoulders. He reached down for the tin cup, and that is when I saw the other man approach the charmer. He nearly shielded the smaller man's aged and bent body with his own taller, stronger build. An exchange of some kind was made, and the bigger man walked away. The snake charmer sighed, as if life itself departed in that breath, and looked into his cup.

"What happened?" I asked. "Why is he so sad?"

"He just had to pay the man who owns this street." Samir gestured to the sidewalk beneath us. "Even the snake charmer has someone to pay. He puts snakes into baskets so comfortable they do not realize they are imprisoned, but the snake charmer, though he looks free, knows he is trapped same as the snakes are."

When I looked at my brother, I found my own sadness for the old man reflected on his face. Samir sighed. "We are all of us snakes and charmers, Jasmina. No one is truly free."

I wanted to tell him that was not true, that I had known people who lived in freedom and shared it with others. But I could not, not without telling him too much and endangering those I loved. As we walked away, I realized with surprise that I felt something new for Samir. For the first time of our lives, I respected him.

twenty-eight
A Visitor

It did not last. The moment we returned to the modeling agency building, Samir roughly escorted me to my room and told me I would remain there until he decided I deserved to come out. I kicked at him, but he shut the door and locked it from the outside. "You're just like him!" I yelled, kicking the door instead. He did not respond, and the sound of his footsteps faded away. I kicked harder and yelled louder.

An hour passed while I paced and muttered to myself, kicking the door each time I walked by it. Eventually a door down the hallway opened. It sounded like the front door. I yelled at Samir again, not lowering my voice even when I heard the lock turn in my door.

I swung the door open and fell over myself. I had planned to shove Samir aside and just leave the building. Maybe I would come back a few days later and give him a few options: he could let me stay, and I would help, but only on my terms. I would get paid for my work and would be free to come and go as I pleased.

The person at the door was not Samir. The garment factory owner filled the space in front of me. I had launched myself forward and had to throw my body to the side to avoid crashing into him.

"How lovely you look today," he said. Either he was deaf and had not heard my wild screeching, or he valued the sight of his eyes over the sound of his ears. It was clear he liked what he saw. "Your cheeks are quite flushed, child. It is most becoming."

I would have run, but he blocked the doorway. "I have brought you a friend," he said, entering the room. I backed away, puzzled now at his intention. If someone was with him, maybe he would refrain from touching my hair or my arm or my chin. Ducking to the side when his hand reached out, I looked behind him and gasped.

"It's you." Fayeed stood in the hallway, eyes lit up with recognition. "Samir's . . . helper. So you're the new girl here."

"Oh, it's you!" A feminine voice caught my attention. Beside Fayeed stood a girl who looked to be about my age, a bright smile on her round face. Her obvious happiness seemed foreign; it felt like forever since I had seen someone genuinely pleased. "I'm so glad to meet you in person," she exclaimed, and then took my hand.

She was speaking to me? "Do . . . I . . . know you?"

Her laugh was high and made her sound very young. "Not in person, of course, but I hoped you would be here. What luck!"

Fayeed ushered her back into the hallway and directed her to a front desk, which must have recently appeared in the waiting area complete with receptionist, because I had never seen it before. Then he turned to Gar. "May I speak with Samir's assistant for a moment, sir?"

The garment factory owner looked nearly as confused as I but nodded his assent and huffed his way from the room, turning in the doorway to say, "Don't talk too long. We have business to take care of."

The door shut with a click, and I turned to Fayeed. "What is going on? Who is that girl, and why does she think she knows me?"

"Jasmina," Fayeed said. "It is Jasmina, right? Come and sit with me a moment."

I thought of how Samir had described him but decided he could not be much worse than Samir himself, and I could handle my brother when I wasn't locked in a room. I sat on the floor next to Fayeed and started in on my questions again.

He put a hand on my knee, and I was so surprised at the touch from a boy I forgot to pull away and simply stared at his hand. What was he doing?

"Jasmina." His hand rubbed circles around my knee, and I watched as hypnotized by the movement as that cobra I'd seen earlier. "You need to understand how things work here."

"Stop that," I ordered, but my voice was only a hoarse whisper. "Don't touch me."

"I know who you are, Jasmina." His voice was soft and a frightening kind of gentle. "If the garment factory owner found out, do you know what he would do to you? He would make you his personal slave, trapped and owned for the rest of your life."

"I'm leaving," I said, scooting away from him and his hand. "I'm going back to the streets. I was a street kid before. I can do it again."

"But you're not a kid any longer, are you?" He put his hand back on my leg, and though I pushed at it, he closed his fingers firmly and would not release me. "How long do you think you would last out there before you were attacked? Or trapped and sold? There are many bad things that can happen to a pretty girl on the streets."

"Please let me go." I was fighting tears, fighting fear and my lack of understanding of what was happening. I pulled and twisted away from his hand until I could stand and run toward the door.

"I know information that could destroy your brother."

My feet halted at his words. "Why should I care?"

"You gave everything you had to find him." Fayeed stood. "Would you let him die?"

I kept my back to him, but my whole body trembled. "What do you mean?"

His voice was close to my ear. "I know Samir set fire to the garment factory. Gar owed the quarry owner money and would not pay, so my boss, the quarry owner, punished him." Fayeed circled me as he spoke. "He convinced Samir to do it. Promised him freedom and even a paying job. So after the fire when my boss conveniently found you both, Samir was willing to go with him, expecting his reward." He chuckled. "Which of course the boss had no intention of giving. You both were made slaves again. How tragic."

His hand reached out and with one finger, he ran a trail across my collarbone and then across my shoulders as he continued to circle, like a predator. "I was a quarry slave too, though you were not there long enough to remember me. After you were sold away, Samir and I made a pact to work together against both men. We used a guard to get a message to Gar, informing him that the boss had burned his building and taken many of his children. He arrived the next day with policemen he had likely bribed, threatening all sorts of evil in retaliation." He chuckled. "Samir and I arranged the partnership. We pacified them both with a nice agreement. Each thinks he is deceiving the other; each thinks he is at the top." He stopped in front of me and breathed the fear in the air as if it were sweet perfume. "The truth is that Samir and I stand at the top, and now that I have you, even he is under my control."

twenty-nine
Deception

"What do you want from me?" My mind dug around like a beggar searching through a trash pile for any way to get away from Fayeed.

He smiled. "I want you. You will belong to me. Do what I say. Tell Samir what I want him to hear." He took a strand of my hair and wrapped it around a finger on his right hand. "And if I come visit you, you will not run away. You will not call for help if I touch you. Anything I want, you will do, for you are mine now."

Where could I run? The streets were dangerous. Gar was dangerous. Even Samir would use me somehow. Was there anyone in the world who was good?

My longing for Asha and Grandmother and Milo and even Dapika filled me to bursting. The bursting part came out in tears. I hated how Fayeed enjoyed watching the proof of my pain, but could not make them stop. He had both hands on my face when someone banged on the door. "You've had enough time, son." It was Gar, and he sounded as impatient as I was afraid. "I'm coming in."

The door opened. I turned and hid my face while Fayeed behind me said smoothly. "This girl has agreed to assist me when Samir does not need her help. I'm going to start training her tomorrow to oversee the new girls."

I felt Gar's eyes on me. "In that case, this new girl can stay with her for now. I'll put the other products in the room across the hall." I turned and saw Gar facing Fayeed. Without speaking, with only their eyes and how they stood, they threatened one another.

Fayeed stood still, eyes hard, but he finally lowered his gaze. "That's a good idea," he said and then looked at me with a sneer. "We wouldn't want her to get lonely. I'll train her next week then."

I was hiding my fear. He hid his hatred. Gar hid his suspicions. We all performed an act, like the snake charmer did.

The girl bounced into the room. "They told me I get to stay with you. How exciting! We'll have such fun." She was at my side, clutching my hand. "They said they'll start taking pictures tomorrow. Some girls have been lucky enough to get chosen by agencies in Europe!"

Relief flooded my whole body when Fayeed left the room, Gar behind him. I rushed to shut the door and pressed my back against it, breathing heavily.

"Are you okay?" the girl asked. "You look like the goddess of death just visited you."

She had no idea how close she was to the truth. "Who are you?" I asked.

As if I played a game, she laughed and waved a hand at me. "I'm Kiya, of course. Do I not look at all like my picture?"

I was tired of all the lies, tired of pretending. "I have no idea who you are. Where would I have seen your picture?"

"On Facebook." Her smile faded. "You're the one who talked me into coming here."

I sunk to the floor. "I've never seen you in my life. And what is a face book?"

"You're telling the truth, aren't you?" The girl, Kiya, stared at me, then at the camera equipment around the room. Her gaze landed on the computer at the desk. "Does that work?"

At my nod, she pulled a plastic chair from a stack and set it in front of the desk, hunting around until she found the button to turn the machine on. We both waited while it whirred and flashed its colors and words. Once a picture of the elephant goddess appeared across the screen along with several documents I knew to be Samir's, she began clicking buttons. Another screen covered the goddess, and there was Kiya's photo, smiling and young and pretty. I stood and approached the desk.

"This is Facebook," she said. She tapped the down arrow, and I saw many pictures and many words. "My parents let me open an account for my birthday. I go to the internet café near our village every weekend and sometimes after school when I'm supposed to be studying."

She started typing into a long white section at the top of the page. I was shocked to see her spell out my name. "How did you know my—?" I stopped midway when my photo appeared right there on the screen. "How did you get my picture?"

"We've been sending each other messages for a week. Do you have a problem with your memory or something? Here, look."

She stood and had me sit in front of the computer. Another screen popped up, and I read aloud cheerful notes of introduction from the modeling agency and then a message from me introducing myself as a seasoned model at the agency. The note gushed about how wonderful it was to work there, how much money I made, and how popular I had become from the modeling. Replies from Kiya were hesitant at first, but my messages convinced her that her life in the village was boring and a life in the city was not only exciting but would keep her independent and away from an arranged marriage. She would meet lots of handsome young men in the city.

"You were right. As soon as I got off the bus, Fayeed was there to meet me. He's so good looking, and since I arrived, he's been so sweet. I'm so glad I came."

I swallowed and choked. Samir had told me once his job was to bring in girls from the streets and Fayeed had the easier job of finding them on the computer. At the time all I had heard was Samir's jealousy, his resentment that not being able to read had forced him to take the harder position. I thought of Fayeed's smooth skin and eyes dark as charcoal. "Fayeed sent these messages to you, not me." I had only whispered, so Kiya kneeled beside me and asked me to repeat my words. "The day I came, Fayeed took my picture with his phone. He's the one who sent you those messages, pretending to be me." I turned and looked hard at her, seeing confusion spread across her face as I spoke. "He is not good or sweet. I don't know what he promised you, but you should not believe him."

"But—but I don't understand." She shook her head, looking back at my photo. "Why would—what—why am I here if—"

I wished I could answer her questions and my own. Was this really a modeling agency at all? Samir said Gar had found a business that was easier and paid more than the garment factory. How could a handful of girls do that? And why had he called them *products*?

"Jasmina." I was still surprised the girl knew my name. She grabbed both my hands. "What is going on here?"

I looked at her and had to tell the truth. "I don't know."

Signing Papers

Early the next morning, Kiya was summoned by a woman who called herself the receptionist. I followed them both to the front area of the building where four other girls sat in chairs and fluttered and giggled like children. "This desk wasn't here when I came," I said to the woman handing out papers for the girls to sign. "Neither were you."

She looked me over. "I only come when a new batch comes in. If you're going to work here, you'd better learn fast to do what you're told and not ask questions."

I looked hard for information in her eyes but found nothing. She was shuttered away like Samir and Fayeed.

Kiya reached for a paper and motioned me to her side. I sat and she asked, "What does it say?"

The woman's words were sharp and quick. "It's just a document saying you will accept a modeling job here. That's why you came, isn't it?" She handed Kiya a pen and looked directly at me. Her eyes were no longer shuttered. They shot a warning.

With a finger I casually pointed out where Kiya was to sign, my eyes scanning the paper. It was, indeed, a statement accepting the job, but there were too many words on the page for me to read before Kiya had signed her name and the woman snatched the sheet away. She added it to the stack, which she promptly put into a drawer of the desk. Then she looked at the girls and smiled. "Welcome to our modeling agency. Come with me, and I will show you the room where we will take your first photos." The girls beamed when she added, "We work with modeling companies around the world. You were chosen especially, and if you do well, you might get an offer from one of our partner companies in Bombay, the Middle East, or even Europe."

The girls stood readily and followed the woman down the hall to the second door on the left. I remained behind. When the door shut and the giggling sound lessened, I rushed to the drawer with the papers and yanked it open. My eyes darted left and right over the page Kiya signed, but the only unusual section I could find was near the bottom where the person signing gave permission to have a passport made, and full authority was given to the agency to keep and maintain the passport.

I slid the paper back onto the stack and shut the drawer. Kiya would need a passport if she did get a job in another country, but why would the agency keep it? Without it, she would never be permitted to return for the promised visits.

My body jerked from the chair when someone rounded the corner and said my name. "Oh, it's you." My hand was at my racing heart. "I thought it was her."

Kiya's smile was back. "Jasmina, have you been in that room? It has colored silk backdrops and special lighting." She clasped her hands in front of her. "This is the most exciting day of my life. The woman already started taking pictures, and my turn will come up soon."

I frowned. "Have you forgotten you were deceived into coming here?" I asked.

"Oh, I told her about that, and she explained everything." Kiya looked out the darkened glass of the windows, not noting how I clutched the desk behind me at her words. The fool. What would Fayeed do when he found out we knew?

She turned back to face me. "She said Fayeed would have sent the messages himself, but he knew we girls would not respond to a man. It would not be appropriate, and I'm glad they understand that. My parents used to warn me about the city, but they were wrong. Fayeed used your photo and name and now is having a woman take the pictures to make sure all of us feel comfortable and safe." She twirled and smiled. "If my parents had wanted to arrange a marriage with someone like him, I might have stayed home."

A sound came from down the hallway. "Oh, they're calling for me." She twirled one more time. "I'll tell you all about it later tonight."

I sat in the nearest chair, too stunned to be angry at Kiya's foolish choice to believe what she wanted to believe. Fayeed did not care about being appropriate, of that I was certain. If this really was a modeling agency with bright possibilities, why were two girls locked in the basement?

When Samir arrived later that afternoon, I kept quiet. What I knew about Fayeed might prove useful, but I was not yet certain how, so I held my questions and my knowledge inside as he turned on the computer and demanded I type an e-mail message for him.

"This is for a partner in Europe, so the message has to be in English." He started dictating, then interrupted himself to say with a scowl, "What is wrong with you? Why are you going so slow?"

I scowled back. "Your English is even worse than mine. I'm fixing it to sound better."

"I don't have time for your one-finger typing," he grumbled behind me. "Go faster."

"Do you want it to make sense to this person or not?"

He crossed his arms. "What does it say? What did you write?"

I spoke the words I had typed. "New shipment of five arrived yesterday. Ready by day following tomorrow. Tell me address to send."

"That sounds good. Now click the button that sends it to him."

He had told me how to send messages the first day, but still felt the need to instruct me on exactly how to do each step. "When are you going to pay me for this work?" I asked.

My brother headed for the door. "Do I look rich? I have to feed you and keep you here. You haven't earned any more than that." He left the room, and I stifled the urge to kick the door again. My foot was still sore from yesterday. Instead I opened the door.

"Samir," I called out, stopping him before he left the building. "What things do you ship to Europe?" They must be valuable if he only shipped five at a time.

"If you ever want money from me, you'll stop asking questions and just do what I say!"

The door to the agency slammed behind him, and I stood staring at it, trying to decide if there was any amount of money in the world worth blindly obeying my little brother.

thirty-one
Only Four Products

I was arguing with Samir over how to arrange English words into a sentence for an e-mail when the squealing came from across the hall. Within a minute, Kiya burst into the room, her cheeks filled out around her gleaming smile, her skin flushed.

"Jasmina, can you imagine what has just happened?" Words gushed from her like the time a portion of our thatch roof broke through and all the monsoon rain poured in. "The receptionist just told us that Mr. Gar sent our photos to his partner agencies around the world, and they heard back from one of the agencies already. Guess which one." She grabbed my hands and pulled me out of the desk chair. "Europe!" She danced us both around in a circle. "Gar is coming to tell us what they said. Oh, Jasmina, this is the best day of my life!"

Such a feeling of revulsion filled me, I could not even pretend to be happy for her. When she skipped from the room, not noticing my silence or my concern, I turned to my brother.

"The girls were photographed as they are. No new clothes. No hairstyling or makeup." I grasped the back of the chair. "And yet an agency in Europe wants them? After one day?"

His mouth pulling down into a frown was not a new sight to my eyes, but this time even his eyes seemed to frown at me. "I've told you not to ask questions, Jasmina. Don't even think. It would not be safe to know the answers you seek."

I heard a door open and then Gar's voice. My hands froze on the chair. "Stay away from him if you can," Samir whispered as he passed me to leave the room. I heard him greet Gar and wondered if my brother was actually speaking out of care for me or only out of concern for his own position. Would my questions truly endanger me or only endanger whatever work he was doing? He might be doing something sourced by Gar or perhaps be stealing from him. Is that why he wanted me to keep quiet about my suspicions?

Fayeed's voice pulled every other thought from my mind. I had to leave the room before he found me there alone. I threw open the door that Samir had closed behind him. Fayeed was there in the doorway, his eyes in slits as he looked at me. I started shaking.

"What a special day this is," Gar announced. I glanced to see him ushering the models into the photo room. "Let's all come together so I can tell you the good news." He turned to Samir. "Where is our receptionist today?"

Samir's answer was too low for me to hear, distracted as I was by Fayeed standing in front of me. I nudged him aside enough to get my body into the hallway just as Samir and Gar followed the girls into the room. The moment the door was shut Fayeed's hands circled my neck and pushed me against the wall.

"The receptionist came to my place last night," he whispered. "She told me you discovered my new little computer method."

"My—photo," was all I could get out. His grasp blocked my air.

"What did you say?" He was smiling, enjoying my desperate clutching at his arms. I began to see dark spots and lost all energy to resist. His hands released me, and I slumped to the ground, gasping for air, my hand at my bruised throat. "Your photo," he said above me. "Your name as well. It is working beautifully." He knelt in front of me and let me see the victory on his face. "Your new friend Kiya would never have come if I'd asked her, but you, Jasmina, so excited and happy, convinced her that all was well." He grabbed a section of my hair and pulled me painfully to my feet. "Anything that happens to her, you helped make happen."

Wincing, I tried to pull away. "You can't—"

The door across the hallway opened and by the time Gar had maneuvered himself through the door, Fayeed's hands were in his pockets and his face a mask of youth and innocence. "I've just been telling Samir's assistant how Facebook works," he said. "She wants to learn more, so she can help me when it's time for her to work with me too."

"That can wait," Gar said, reaching into a pocket and removing a handkerchief. He wiped sweat from his forehead and temples. "Right now I need you to go in the room and talk to those girls. They like you better than me. Go tell them about Europe."

Fayeed took in a deep breath, his hatred for Gar clear to anyone watching, which Gar was not. "Yes, sir." He turned to me, and I shrank back. "We'll finish our talk later."

I gave plenty of room as he passed by me and entered the room. Soon girls were squealing again. Gar wiped his face again and chuckled. He looked at me. "Don't you wish you could go to Europe too?"

My eyes did not lower as I shook my head. His chuckle died. "You really do look familiar," he said. "Were you ever—"

Kiya swung open the door and threw her arms around me. "We're going to Europe!" she exclaimed, bouncing up and down. Other girls followed her until a clump of chattering female conversation filled the hallway. "We leave the day after tomorrow."

"So soon." I looked at Gar again, who was still staring at me, his brows together. "That's unusual, don't you think?"

Kiya glanced back at Gar, and he arranged his face into a benevolent smile. "Well, not when the girls are as beautiful as these are," he said loudly, his smile broadening when Kiya and the others giggled. "Now all of you get plenty of rest tonight. We'll take you out to get passports made tomorrow. Then after that is the big day, and we want you to look your best."

He waved a hand over them like a king blessing his subjects, and they twittered and fluttered behind and around him until he had exited the building. Fayeed, still in the hallway, came to stand close behind me. "You will regret any word you say to your brother about any of this," he hissed. An object, small, round, and cold, pressed against my back, and my breath again escaped me. When it pulled away and he left, I longed for a place to curl into a ball and cry. Instead I listened to Kiya and the other girls talk about how wonderful their new lives would be until I could stand it no more. I fled back to my room only to find Samir there, clicking on the computer keyboard. He slammed his fist against the desk, and I jumped.

He saw me. "Get over here," he said.

"You could ask politely," I offered.

"There's a new e-mail. Read it to me."

Still feeling a little lightheaded, I sat at the desk, finding my curiosity greater than my irritation. I wrapped my hand over the small round object and moved it to make the arrow click on the new message. It appeared, and I read the message aloud. "Send only four products. One buyer backed out. Address below." I read the address which was in Europe and then jerked from my place when Samir slammed his fist into the desk again with a curse. I stood and faced him. "What are you selling that is so valuable? Are you working with Gar or do you work against him somehow?"

"Shut the computer down," he ordered. He started to say more, but Kiya wandered into the room, holding her orna out and twirling so the material floated out behind her like a kite. With one last angry glare at the computer, he marched past Kiya, ignoring her completely, and left the room.

Kiya watched him go. "He must want to go to Europe too and feels jealous," she remarked, draping her orna over herself and practicing various poses. "It's odd. I thought it took weeks to get a passport, but Gar says we'll have ours by tomorrow evening. He must have connections in high places."

Or low places, I wanted to say. How could I find out what was really going on?

thirty-two
The End of a Lie

I had stayed up half the night, trying to search through Samir's e-mail messages without clicking anything that would let him know I had spied on him. I found more notes about products, but nothing that told me more than I already knew. Once I gave up on that search, my terror of Fayeed kept me from sleeping several more hours. I had to get away from here, and very soon. But I needed money. Whatever Samir was selling was worth a large sum, but he obviously had no intentions of sharing.

And how could I leave Kiya and the others behind when I was certain what was promised to them could not be as good as it seemed?

Sometime before the night was over, I fell asleep. My groggy senses became aware at some point during the morning that more than one male arrived and had taken the girls to get their passports, but once the building was silent again, I gladly resumed my slumber. I must have slept most of the day away for I woke to the sound of the girls returning, and when I looked out the window, the light had dimmed already, and hundreds of crows, beaks open wide with unpleasant caws, flew from the city as they did every evening.

"Come into the photo room, all of you," I heard a masculine voice say. It was either Gar or Samir. Fayeed's voice was smoother than that. "I have an important announcement."

I sat enjoying the silence for a minute or two until the door burst open and Kiya threw herself into the room, hands over her face. She dropped to the floor next to me and sobbed. "It's not fair!" she wailed.

I sat up and rubbed my weary eyes. "What is it?"

"They won't let me go." Her words spilled out with her tears. "He just told us the agency said they only needed four girls, not five, so I would have to wait until the next time. Why me?" she blurted out. "This is the worst day of my life!"

Kiya likely sought for sympathy from me, but I had none to give. I sat like a concrete block there next to her, so full of sudden awareness I felt as heavy as one and as useless.

It was the girls. They were the products in the e-mails. Samir and Gar and Fayeed—all of them were trading people for money. I thought of Samir telling me all the lies Gar put in place to convince my parents to take a job that made them into slaves. I thought of how Gar had promised Father free education for us, and we ended up forced to work without pay in a garment factory.

How much easier Gar had it now. He had Samir to find runaway girls on the streets and Fayeed to find discontent girls on the computer, and all he needed was a place to keep them and a lie to feed them until someone was willing to buy.

Slavery had to be at the end of his lie. I had to get us all out—tonight—money or no money. But how could I convince Kiya and the others? They would never believe me.

Kiya had curled herself into a corner, crying about her bad luck. I brought my knees up to my chest and wrapped my arms around them, pondering the multitude of terrible possibilities that Kiya should be crying over but as yet did not even know about. I thought of Fayeed and the terrifying ownership in his eyes. I thought of Samir and how he said if they got me, he would not sacrifice to save me. I thought of Gar and the quarry owner and the girls in the basement.

"The girls in the basement!" My arms flailed wide. I stood and grabbed Kiya, pulling her to stand with me. "Are they all gone for the night?" I asked.

"Who?" She rubbed her arm where I'd grabbed her.

"Gar, Fayeed, Samir. Whoever was here."

Her tears subsided. "I think so. They always leave before dark, to keep things appropriate."

I kicked the desk chair, resisting the urge to kick her. If she believed that, this was going to be even harder than I thought. "Come with me." I ran across the room to the door, Kiya behind me asking questions. I yanked the door open, glad Samir had finally stopped locking it at night, and ran down the hallway to the end.

"What? What is it?" she gasped as we stood facing the wall.

I slammed my fist against the wall, knocking hard so I would sound like Samir had, confident and expecting a response.

"What are you doing? This isn't a door."

The wall moved, and Kiya put a hand over her open mouth when the section slid away and revealed the set of stairs.

"Come on," I said, leading the way down into the darkness.

thirty-three
The Basement

"What's down here? Jasmina, I'm really scared."

I was too but would not admit it.

"What if there are rats?"

Fayeed's words came to mind. "Don't worry. The rats you need to fear all stay upstairs."

"What?"

I had reached the bottom step. Feeling around, but not touching the string to pull the light switch, I whispered into the darkness, "Can someone turn on the light? We need to talk with you."

Kiya clutched my orna behind me. We waited in silence for what seemed a long time. A swift rush of air breezed past, the light came on, and the air rushed past in the opposite direction. I had seen no one.

"I know there are two of you down here, and I need to talk with you. Please."

Nothing.

"There are four girls upstairs who think they are going to Europe to be models."

I heard a sniff from one direction. A sound of disbelief from another.

"Why would they put anyone down here?" Kiya asked me. I turned and saw her squinting beyond the border of light, though she did not stray one step away from where I stood.

"We're here to be punished."

Both of us jumped at the sound. I swung around and looked to my left, where the voice had come from, and gradually my eyes adjusted enough to see a woman, maybe just a girl, rise from where she had been crouching on the floor. She took a step toward us, and I fought the urge to cover my nose to block the smell.

"How long have you been here?" Kiya's words, accented by horror, filled the room.

"Thirteen days."

"Why did they put you down here?"

The one girl I could see came closer, and the smell came with her. "We came to get jobs as models, like the advertisement said."

"I met a boy who told me I was beautiful," said another voice. "He convinced me to come."

Kiya shuddered behind me. Or maybe it was me. Samir's face came to mind. Had he put them here?

The first girl walked around us, much like Fayeed had done earlier. "How did you know we were down here?"

Watching her made me dizzy, which mixed with my nausea at the stench, not to mention the whole situation itself, had me wanting to run upstairs and forget my need for answers. Did they have any way to go to the bathroom down here?

The girl came to stand in front of me. "You came down here before. With him."

I nodded. "I've been typing e-mails for him. About products for Europe."

The second voice, belonging to the girl still hidden, started crying. "Products. That's all we are to them."

Nausea that had filled my stomach rose to my throat. The girl in front of me smirked, and her words were far more rank than her scent. "That was my job once they found out I could read and knew a little English. When I figured out what was really happening here and tried to leave, they put me in the basement." She stepped nearer. "He's waiting for me to break. Or die."

From the corner the crying sounds increased.

I could still see only the one girl, her eyes wild and her hair as matted and tangled as mine had been when I lived on the streets. "When will you give in?" I asked. It was not meant to be a cruel question. I could think of nothing else to say. My mind felt numb.

"I will not," she answered. "I have no family to threaten. He got me off the streets. I've begged and stolen and sold discarded trash. But I will not help him sell girls as slaves." She looked at Kiya. "They will go to Europe, but they will never become models."

Kiya whimpered against my shoulder. "I want to go home."

"You'll never see home again," the voice in the darkness said like a village prophet pronouncing our doom.

"Why did you get sent here?" I asked the darkness.

A sniff, then shuffling. I squinted but still could not see her. "I ran away from home and ended up on the streets." Her voice sounded young. "He found me and was nice to me. I trusted him when he said he could give me a safe place to stay." She started crying again. "I miss my mother."

The girl facing me crossed her arms. "She was brought in to clean the building and run errands. After the first batch of new girls disappeared to the Middle East and then another group was flown to Bombay, I realized what was happening, and we both tried to escape." She touched her stringy hair. "We've been here ever since."

"I've never seen them bring you food or anything." Kiya whispered.

"They don't whenever new girls are here." Her smirk reappeared. "But they are never here for more than a few days."

Kiya grasped my arm. "Fayeed is coming in the morning to take the girls to the airport." Her words brought me out of my trance and into a moment of decision. I had to act. If my brother was partly responsible for this, I had to do something to reverse it.

"By the time Fayeed gets here, we'll all be gone," I said. "Come with me, both of you. I know a place where you can go for help, if you promise me you will tell no one where you are going."

"It won't work," the girl said. "You'll just end up down here with us."

"And we'll be killed," the second voice wailed. "He said they'd kill us if we tried to get out again."

"No one is going to get killed." I fueled my voice with confidence even as I shuddered. Not looking back I started up the stairs. At the top only Kiya was with me. "Come to the bottom of the stairs," I commanded. Though I inserted the authority I'd heard in Samir's voice into my own, I was still surprised when two small clumps of humanity gathered below, both girls' eyes up on me. The second girl looked as young as she had sounded.

"Listen to me," I said. "I'm leaving this place. If we go now, we'll have all the night hours to flee before they even realize we are gone. By the time they start searching, we will all be safe in a place they know nothing about." I would take them to the compound and the missionaries. It would mean facing my humiliation and shame, but I would take them in, plead for mercy for these victims and then face the condemnation and punishment I deserved. It could not be worse than what waited for me here. "This is your only chance. Will you come with me?"

The girls looked at each other but did not move. "I have no time to convince you," I said. "I'm going. You can come with me or remain behind."

117

I turned and walked out the basement door and started down the hall, unconcerned about making noise, glad that Samir, Fayeed, and Gar all stayed elsewhere. They must have known the new girls would need no locked doors to keep them inside. After all, the sign above the front door said they would give girls their dreams. Before they became nightmares.

"They're coming," Kiya said, looking behind us. I did not turn until Kiya and I stood outside the door housing the four other girls. "Talk quickly," I told her. She rushed inside, and I heard her fast words and their arguments of disbelief. I turned to the two basement girls. "We must leave soon" was all I needed to say. When they went inside, I heard gasps. Within five minutes all of them were in the hallway with me. Kiya, four terrified clean girls, and two terrified dirty ones.

I led the way to the front of the building. It would be difficult, sneaking through the city with such a large group without leaving a trail, but I had lived on the street and still remembered a few of the old skills.

We reached the door. I waited until the girls were all close enough for me to whisper, "Stay within sight of me and do not speak."

They nodded, and I pulled the door. It did not open.

It was locked. From the outside.

thirty-four
Trapped

The sounds of panic behind me echoed in my ears. I yanked on the door. It would not budge. I looked for some kind of lever or button or keyhole.

"We're trapped!" Kiya was near hysteria.

"We have to get back to the basement before he comes in the morning!" a girl cried. "He'll kill us all if he sees us up here!"

"Hush," I warned. "Give me a minute to think."

The girls quieted, but their jittery hands and eyes were impossible to ignore. "Sit down against the wall. No, don't. You're filthy." There was a tiny washroom connected to the room where I stayed. "Kiya, take them into our room and get them cleaned up. The rest of you go wait there. I'll be there in a few minutes."

Kiya, less hysterical now that she had something to do, herded the girls toward the room. I stayed at the door, searching over and around it for some way to pry it open. I checked the windows to see if I could break them, but they were lined with steel bars. We were prisoners.

I ran back to the room and looked all around me for an idea, a tool, anything. My gaze crossed over the computer desk, cameras, and metal poles with strange equipment attached at the end. I went to the stack of poles and pulled one upright. It was heavy, but too tall to be used as a weapon.

If Fayeed arrived first in the morning, I could think of no outcome that was not horrible. I prayed Samir would come before the others. Though it would mean he was more evil than I ever imagined, it would also mean there was a small chance the girls could escape.

I pulled Kiya aside. "Remember that place on the computer where Fayeed was pretending to be me?"

"On Facebook?"

I nodded. "Can you click the things that will make that come on the computer again?" How I wished I had learned about Asha and Mark's computer when I lived with them. "Can you send a message to Fayeed?"

She visibly shook. "Why would I want to do that?"

"We need to keep him from being the first one to get here tomorrow." Kiya pushed buttons and typed words and, like magic, there was my picture again with excited words about becoming a model and being popular. "Is it possible to send him a message from someone other than you? I want you to tell him you want to be a model, and you came to the city, but you got lost and can't find the building."

"Um . . . I have a school friend who has an account, and I know her password. I could send it from her." She clicked something, and a stranger's photo appeared.

This must be how Samir felt all the time, having words around him but not being able to read. I had no understanding of passwords or accounts, but I nodded, hoping whatever Kiya said meant my idea would work. I told her the place to say where she waited, near the quarry. I did not know where we were, but I did remember that it took a while to get here from the quarry, so that should keep him away for at least some of the morning, if he read it before coming here.

We were a ragged army as the dawn rose, waiting crouched below the windows, our eyes peeking out above the sill. I had shared my plan, and it was weak at best. If Samir came, he would come to my room first, giving us our opportunity. If Fayeed came, he might go to the girls' room first, or he might come to mine. I trembled at the memory of his hand on my leg. If I guessed the wrong room and we were all waiting in the other room, he would be suspicious and that would not aid us at all. Had we left the basement door open, that would have been perfect. He would have gone in to see what happened, and we could have shut the door and barred it. Unfortunately, no one had thought of that at the time.

I thought of one more thing. "Kiya, go back to the room and get on the computer. Go to that face book thing, and find every girl he sent a message to. Then you send them a message and tell them the truth." She started toward the room, and I called after her, "And take my picture and my name off there."

"Here he comes."

I turned sharply. Legs. Arms. The face was hidden by a rickshaw awning. He walked around the rickshaw.

"It's Samir." What relief. "Run to the room."

Metal poles dropped to the ground, and we all fled. Had it been Fayeed, my only strategy had been to grab him the moment he came inside the front door and with our combined weight hold him down, drop the heavy poles on him, and have the biggest girls sit on him while the rest escaped. I had given the compound address to the girls and teamed them up in groups of two. It was risky, sharing the address, but I knew I could not tell them while Fayeed was there, and if he were the man arriving, I knew I would be the last girl to go and might not make it away.

We were all in danger, myself most of all, for what none of the other girls knew and I would not tell them was the fact that Samir always wore a hidden knife, but Fayeed carried a gun.

We waited in the room, breathless, as Samir took his time coming down the hallway. "Remember the address?" I whispered. "Remember your partner?" I got nods in response and turned my attention to the door, which was opening.

"Jasmina, what are all the poles doing out—"

My yell set off a chain reaction of screams. We grabbed Samir and pulled him to the ground, our weapon of surprise proving strong. He looked around as if counting the girls. It must have been a shock, seeing eight girls when the night before only six had been upstairs.

We wrapped his hands behind his back using electrical cords, and just for added safety, I sat on his chest. "Go, all of you," I said. Only Kiya hesitated. The rest ran.

"Kiya, go. I'll find you later."

"Promise?" Her eyes were filled with tears.

"I promise." It was an easier lie than many I had told.

She looked back one more time and then followed the others. The building went from shrill voices to silence. I sat on my struggling brother, allowing myself one moment to feel a sense of victory that at least they had escaped his hands.

"Jasmina, how could you? Don't you know I'll get killed for this?"

His voice carried the wounded sound of the betrayed. I slapped his arrogant face. "How could I? How could you? How could you put girls in that basement? How could you sell people as slaves? Call them products?"

I could not even speak of the acts he called his job. "I wish you were not my brother."

thirty-five
Running Again

Samir whined and complained until I was ready to bang my head against a concrete wall, or his. I tasted blood and told myself to stop biting my lip as I tried to develop a new plan. Thus far, I had only thought of getting the girls out, not beyond. After five minutes in which I could think of nothing other than returning to the compound and begging forgiveness—which I had once again decided I could not do without all the money I stole—I spoke to my brother.

"Listen to me, and I will let you go." He stopped squirming, and I stood and faced him, hoping looking down on him from above would help put status to my words. "I am leaving. All of this. I will never be part of it. If you want me to leave without exposing you to anyone and everyone I can think of, you will do as I say. I need money. A lot of it. All the rupees Fayeed stole from me. I don't care if you have to steal it back from him. You will get it to me."

"What do you need money for?" he grunted, trying to maneuver into a sitting position, his hands still tied behind his back with the cord. "If you're on the streets, you'll lose it the first night."

"I'll use it to go free our parents," I said with disdain for the fact that such an idea did not even come to his mind. If there was enough left, I would take it back to Asha. If not, I would find some way to earn the rest. Even if it took me years, I would repay my debt.

"You don't even know where they are."

I slammed my foot against his chest, knocking him flat onto the floor again. "That's why you're going to tell me. Right now. And I will—"

A noise interrupted me, some kind of song playing in the room. I looked around in confusion, but Samir just gave me that look that said he still thought I was a simpleton, and said, "It's my cell phone. In my pocket."

I knelt and pulled the phone out. A picture of Fayeed was on the front, flashing in and out. "Oh no." I opened the phone and pushed a green button. Before I could even hold it up to Samir's ear, Fayeed was yelling. The blood drained from my face. He had followed the directions on the computer message Kiya sent and waited for no one. Now he was back in his room and looking at his computer. He saw her messages telling all the girls the truth. Fury pulsed through the phone in my hand.

"Meet me at the modeling agency," he shouted. "Now. Your sister is going to pay for this, and you're going to watch."

The phone went silent, and Fayeed's picture disappeared.

"What did you do?" Samir's voice held no arrogance now, only fear.

I reached behind him and took the knife he kept hidden. "We have to go. There's no way you can steal that money back from Fayeed now."

"There never was. All your money went to drugs and drink the first night he had it. He's not stupid enough to keep cash around waiting for someone to take it."

As much as I wanted to leave him there, tied up and helpless, I could not. Our mother would be disappointed in me if

I did, and though I no longer hoped for a loving acceptance from my father, I could not bear the thought of his hatred knowing I could have rescued my brother and didn't. Samir's face, white and wide-eyed, told me he fully expected Fayeed to kill him if he found him there.

"Will you get me money?" I asked, my hands on the cords binding him.

"I know of a place. I'll take you there."

It was not much of a promise, but I unwound the cords and moved back as he stood. He reached up to hit me, but I held out his knife in my hand. "You will never strike me again," I said. How did I get to the point that I would hold a weapon toward my own brother? "I will call on every god and goddess above India to punish you for what you have done."

He surprised me by swatting the knife away with a scowl. He passed around me and ran from the room, me following behind him as he said, "They won't bother. They're too busy with their own schemes. Haven't you heard the stories? They lie and cheat and steal each other's lovers. Why should they punish me, when they are worse?"

At his words, bits of truth slammed against me like a swarm of flies. What he said was true. How could they bring justice if they did not live by justice themselves? How could they cleanse me if they were dirty too?

I wanted to think on this more, but Samir threw open the door, and we both ran through and collided with Gar, his wide belly stretching in front of both of us, his thick arm wrapped around Kiya's neck. She struggled, her small fingers clawing against the flesh squeezing her throat.

"Oh, Kiya." I backed two steps away. "Why didn't you run?"

Tears paved wet paths down her cheeks. "I was worried he would hurt you. You said you would come, so I decided to wait."

"Right in front of the building?" Samir put hands on his hips and looked at me. "She's even more naïve than you are."

125

"Why is this girl out of the building?" Gar asked Samir, who dropped his hands from his hips. "What's going on?"

I watched Samir's eyes shift all around. Fayeed was nowhere in sight. Yet.

"Sir, I have discovered a new way to make money, more money and faster." He approached Gar, eyes still looking around, and spoke low into his ear. I strained to listen, but Kiya was crying, and I only heard the words *hotel* and *American*.

I longed to run free of the whole place and everything about it, including Samir. But I needed the money, and I could not leave Kiya to suffer for what I had done. I reached into Grandmother's bag, which I had thought to bring with me as a way to conceal Samir's knife. If Gar had a gun, which was likely, my little knife would be ridiculously inadequate. What could I do?

My shock was great when Gar nodded at Samir, clapped him on the shoulder, and commended his work. He released Kiya and apologized for any distress he caused.

What had Samir told him? I asked him as we began to walk away, but he looked to our left, yelled, "He's coming!" and sprinted toward the road at the end of the alley.

Turning, I saw Fayeed stepping down from a rickshaw. When he saw me and then Samir, he began running toward us, shouting. A glance back and I saw Gar coming back out of the building, also shouting and red faced. He must have gone to the basement. Gar did not run, but he did pull out that gun I had expected he had.

"Run, Kiya!" I cried out. We sprinted with Samir toward a taxi. A driver, obviously used to this area, had seen the situation and pulled up beside the road ahead. He jumped out, engine still running, and opened both side doors.

A shot rang out behind us. I thought I had been running as quickly as I could, but being shot at for the first time in my life got my legs and arms moving even faster. The driver had just returned to his place behind the wheel. Samir jumped into the front passenger seat. I threw myself into the backseat and quickly slid across to make room for Kiya.

Another shot. "Kiya!" I screamed. Blood spurted from her leg, and she fell.

thirty-six
Samir's Plan

Ignoring my fear that another bullet would find its mark, I pulled myself back across the seat and reached out to drag Kiya into the taxi. "Go! Go!" I shouted the moment she was inside. Samir reached back to shut Kiya's door, and the car jerked forward and away. I looked back. Fayeed stopped at the side of the road. His mouth had stopped shouting threats, but his eyes promised worse ones as we slid into the traffic of buses, autos, rickshaws, and other taxis.

"We have to get Kiya to a hospital," I said, still breathless.

"Don't be a fool. That's the first place they'll look for us." Samir shifted to see where Kiya sprawled across the back seat, grimacing in pain, her hand bloody where she grasped her lower leg. "It's a minor wound. Just wrap her orna around it and get it to stop bleeding."

The taxi driver said something to Samir about a higher rate if we got blood on his seat. Samir cursed at him, and they argued back and forth.

"What did you tell Gar that convinced him to let Kiya go free?" I asked, raising my voice to get his attention.

He looked back at us again. "I told him I'd been contacted by a couple of rich foreigners who were looking for some fun. They would pay extra if I brought two girls to them at a hotel immediately."

He shrugged, as if the idea of selling his sister was an everyday event to him. His next words revealed it might as well have been. "If it were true, I'd take you right now. You have ruined what I spent years building up. I can't even go back to get my stuff, not until I have enough money to convince them I sold all the girls in the basement as well as you."

"I'm not going to apologize for getting all of us out of there."

"I have no interest in getting your sympathy." He was scowling again. I sniffed just to irritate him. "What I need is money. A whole lot more than you wanted. There's only one place I know where we can get that kind of money that quickly."

"Where?"

"You deal with her leg and keep it from bleeding on the seat. I'll handle getting the money." He turned back around away from me. "In two days I'll tell you the address where you can go find our parents. Kiya can go home or wherever, and I will get my job back."

We rode in silence except for Kiya's muffled cries as I bound her leg with her orna. Samir was right; it was a minor wound. The bullet grazed her leg rather than entering it, which resulted in much blood but little danger. "It's going to be okay," I whispered to her.

"Jasmina," she whispered back, "I can't go home. I ran away to come here, shamed my family in the community. If I go back, they'll all think I'm . . . that I . . . that my virtue is gone. No one will want to marry me now."

"I thought you didn't want an arranged marriage."

She sniffed and wiped her nose with her sleeve. "Anything would be better than this. People wanting to sell me, trying to kill me. If I can't go home, what am I going to do?"

I tied the orna tight and sat back against the seat. My reassurances to her were meager and fragile, like my old bamboo home had been against the cyclone that washed it out to sea. I had little hope Samir would actually give us any money, much less let us leave freely. He had a plan, but it was certain to benefit him rather than us. I, however, had learned much over the past five or so days. I was no longer as gullible as he supposed, and he was not the only one capable of deceit.

Even so, as the taxi drove on, again passing that section that felt mysteriously familiar, I thought of the snake charmer's show. If I proved to be the snake, Samir would want me in a basket, comfortable but trapped. If I was the charmer, he was the man waiting for me to hand over what I had made.

Snake or charmer, if my brother had his way, I knew I would never be free.

thirty-seven
My Last Letter

Dear Mother,

You have now heard my story. We arrived here where Samir arranged for both Kiya and me to exchange our kidneys for a large sum of money that he says he will split between the three of us. I know he has no such intention. That is why I arranged with the doctor to schedule our operations at different times. If Kiya and I were both unconscious, I know Samir would take the payment and leave. Kiya's operation was earlier today—or rather yesterday as the darkness is nearly ready to give way to the dawn. I will go in today and get the money for Kiya's kidney. Samir wants it all, but Kiya and I have agreed on a secret place to hide most of it. She can retrieve it after she heals. After I hide her portion, I will give the rest to Samir. He will be unhappy about the amount, but will have no choice but to accept it if he wants any of the money from my kidney as well. We promised the doctor a special tip if he released the money only to us.

Oh, Mother, how have I come to this? How can I bear to have you read these words and know what has become of your children? I want to blame everything on Father, on being sold, on Samir, on evil men and women or gods and goddesses who prey on the innocent. But I know that everything that has happened has merely released the darkness already in my own heart. I was horrified once to hear Samir wish revenge on our father and others. Now I find myself wishing I could bring pain and suffering to my brother, so I am no better.

I expected Kiya to return by now. They must be keeping her in the operating room as she recovers. I know little of what happens inside that room, which is as they want it. I could be called at any moment now and will be made to sleep. I will wake up where?

The morning light slips through the window bars and dances across me where I sit. I think through childhood memories of mornings when we were together, when the light sifted through the cracks in the bamboo walls, announcing the morning and waking us to the salty air and the promise of much work and perhaps a little time to read and learn, or imagine myself away someplace exciting.

I have one last regret—that I was unable to get your address to tell the basement girls. They could have told Amrita, and she could have worked with the missionaries to find you and set you free. I know Samir will not take this book to you. I wanted to believe he would because I had no other option, but he is selfish and cruel. He would burn my words or discard them on a trash heap, not bothering even to burn them.

Because I know this, I have thought of one last plan. Amrita's salon is not far from here. I realized just hours ago that is why the place we passed felt familiar. Amrita showed me a picture of it once. I will give this book to Kiya. If I die in the operation, she can take it to Amrita. I cannot hope she or the missionaries would want to find my parents after I stole and lied, so I will ask Kiya to tell them you are her parents instead. Then you will be freed, and Kiya could become a new daughter you could be proud of.

Mother, whatever happens, when you finish reading this, will you offer a prayer for me wherever I am? What

Samir said about the gods and goddesses fills me with despair. I do not ask their help, for they have none to give. However, the missionaries will tell you of Jesus. He is good and holy and set apart from all evil. In my shame, I know I do not deserve His mercy, but my fear compels me to beg for it regardless. I have no pride left, only need. Will you ask Jesus to forgive me? I know if I am to face the unknown place that is death, He is my only hope.

Amrita once said she could not follow Jesus because she could not give up her hate. I have nothing left that I would not throw at His feet, even all of myself, if I could . . . if I had anything left that was acceptable.

I do not know what else to write, how to end this. What does one say when such words may be the last? I should say what I never thought to say when we were together. What was unsaid in cooking together and learning to read and in our stolen moments when we acted out the stories and laughed at ourselves. What never needed to be said then, but needs to be said now.

I love you, Mother. And I'm sorry.

thirty-eight
Still Here

I had finished the letter to my mother and sat silent, full of fear and thinking of death. When the door finally opened, though I had been waiting to be summoned, I still felt the terror grip me, even more so when it was the doctor himself who appeared. He looked at the girl still sleeping on her mat and then motioned to me without a word. I stood and followed, wondering if Samir knew it was time for my operation and was lurking somewhere, waiting to snatch the money away. I might have to bribe the doctor extra in case Samir had offered him more so the doctor would pay him instead.

I walked down a dimly lit corridor to a room curtained off. The doctor drew the curtain aside, and I went in. Two tables stretched across the room, the hard surfaces covered with sheets that once may have been white but now were a mottled grey, stained dark in far too many places. Overhead hung an electric lamp, the plug draped over to a wall where it was secured with tape. A smaller table showcased knives and metal instruments that shone silver in the light. The doctor pulled two strange items from a box, and I watched in fascination as he pulled them onto his hands. They stretched and stretched to cover his fingers and his hands with a layer of plastic-like substance. He put a mask over his mouth and nose and asked, "Are you ready to get started?"

A woman entered, and the doctor said she was his nurse. She wore a sari, which surprised me as I expected her to be in some kind of uniform. She tucked a strand of hair behind her ears and then sneezed into her hand. I waited for her to excuse herself to wash her hands, but she did not.

He gestured for me to lie on the table closest to the curtain. The other table I had assumed was piled with sheets or laundry, covered over with a cloth. However, when I approached, curiosity overcame me, and I put my arm out just enough to make it look accidental as it brushed the cloth aside.

I gasped when the cloth slid aside to reveal two small feet. "There's a person on here!" I said.

"Go get the anesthesia," the doctor told the nurse, who rushed from the room.

The cloth slid more and I saw a partially healed wound on the leg. "Oh no," I whispered. The doctor ordered me not to touch the cloth anymore. I ignored him and pulled the sheet from the body. "Oh, Kiya." They had not even bothered to clothe her. A huge jagged line ran across the skin of her midsection, puffed and red, slashed with X marks where the gash had been stitched with what looked like dirty string. Her eyes were closed. Her face white. "You killed her!"

The nurse returned and handed the doctor a large needle filled with some kind of liquid. He tapped the part encasing the liquid and then pushed the bottom up until some spurted out through the needle. "I didn't, but the infection will. It's just a matter of time." He looked at me and shrugged, but then, perhaps seeing my face and realizing I was next in line, said reassuringly, "It happens sometimes, but don't worry. You look healthy." He looked over at Kiya. "We sedated her so she wouldn't feel any pain."

"You mean you sedated her so she wouldn't scream and bring the police!" I cried.

"The police?" He started toward me with the needle. "The police get plenty of money to allow me to do my work here." The mask distorted as his cheeks filled out behind it into a smile. "You know all about bribes. You shouldn't be surprised."

He reached for my arm. I ran, putting Kiya's table between us.

"Your brother knows about bribes too," he said, stepping casually toward me, unconcerned, as if I was easy prey. "He already has the money for this girl's kidney. And once she dies, he'll get paid much more for the rest. Other pieces and parts of her are worth a great deal."

I forced myself not to throw up. I had to keep focused, think clearly. My dash toward the curtained door was blocked by the woman I now knew was no nurse at all, just as this was no doctor. He was a butcher.

There was no escape. I threw my head back and cried for help. Not from police. Not from my brother. From the only power I knew to be greater than evil. As the needle plunged into my struggling flesh, I cried out, "Jesus, if You can hear me, save me please!"

thirty-nine
My Rescue

Amrita said she was running down the corridor, searching the rooms when she heard my cry. By the time she entered the room with a group of international workers who had been searching for the source of the black market organ trade, I was losing consciousness and thought I was seeing a hallucination. Amrita says I should say a vision as she would rather be a vision than a hallucination, but it matters not because she was really there.

The man and woman about to slice into my body tried to flee but were caught. I do not know what will happen to them and do not care, so long as they are never near me again. Amrita says the international workers, who looked like a bowl of mixed seeds for all their different colors, would be sure to bring them to justice. They had been partnering with the missionaries and Amrita for months, seeking where the operations were taking place, where the organs came from. Now two of them, a man and woman who were from another country but of Indian descent, were back in that room pretending to be the doctor and nurse with others hiding throughout the building and surrounding area in hopes of also catching those who came to pick the organs up and ship them away. I offered to return and pretend to be their patient, but Amrita told me I had been asleep for hours, and she did not trust me to stand upright, much less help in an arrest.

I am fortunate that I only have the effects of the shot to recover from, unlike Kiya, who is suffering beside me in this small space. The moment it is dark outside, we are taking her to the compound where a doctor—a real doctor, one of the missionaries—is waiting to help her, but we cannot go during the day. On the other side of this door, Amrita's salon is open and full of customers. How they sneaked us in here I do not know, but I know with Kiya's feverish skin and inability to walk, if we tried to leave now we would be seen and not only increase our own danger of being found, but destroy the work Amrita is able to do with her beauty shop as cover.

It cannot be risked, but still I long to rush Kiya toward help. I fear she may die before nightfall. She is now clothed, but my mind can still see where they cut her like an animal in the market. How many had died on that table? How close had I been to becoming the next one?

Snakes and charmers. Did Samir organize to have both of us killed? Would he stoop that low to protect his job? If he had no regret destroying other girls' lives, I had to assume he would not regret destroying mine. I will pray for him. And for myself, that I may stop despising him.

I wish I knew what time it was. It feels as if days have passed. When we get to the compound tonight, I will tell Dapika and Milo everything. They deserve my honesty as thanks for saving my life. It was those two friends who came to Amrita. The girls from the basement had flocked to the compound, their desperate fear making their stories most convincing. When they mentioned me, Milo asked so many questions Dapika had to interrupt him just to let the girls answer.

"That was a sneaky trail of lies you left behind," Amrita told me earlier after I woke up. Through the tiny crack she had left in the sliding door leading to our hiding place, large enough to let in some air but not enough for anyone to notice, I saw her standing just a few steps away, tucking stray hairs back as she looked straight at the wall beside the sliding door. I assumed a mirror hung on that wall, though the crack was too small for me to see it. That first time she checked, she told me about Milo and Dapika, and how they had rushed there, so worried, asking her to help find me.

I am humbled at their care. They do not know yet how little I deserve it.

"But how did you know I was getting an operation?" I asked the second time Amrita stopped near the door and slipped a *chapatti* inside for me.

"That was no easy discovery," she said, gesturing toward a bottle of shampoo in her assistant's hand, as if discussing it. "We spent all of last night meeting with my contacts across the city. We started with what the girls who escaped from the modeling agency could tell us about that location. From there we had a time hunting information without giving away that we were searching for you specifically. Finally we were approached by a taxi driver who said he had helped a young man and two young women escape from the building. One had been shot." She laughed a little. "He was hoping for a reward and was quite adamant that the young man had not paid him enough money, considering he had risked his life."

"I'll work for you until I repay whatever you gave him," I said.

"No need. The team reimbursed me, since finding you helped them find the organ doctor." A customer asked a question, and she had to leave then, but the next time she stopped by she told me that the taxi driver had taken her to the building where I was. She had called the international team to meet her there. They were searching inside when I yelled.

"So I have the taxi driver to thank for my life," I commented, my hand resting on Kiya's forehead. Her fever was worse.

"It would seem so, though I am inclined to think the One who saved you was the One you called on." Amrita walked away, telling a woman they could add a haircut to her henna dye job for a discount.

My arms ran with shivers. Was it Jesus who rescued me? I wished I could ask Him why. Since I could not, but on the chance that He had, indeed, heard and helped, I prayed and asked mercy for Kiya, the friend who now lay dying because she had waited for me.

Forty

Returning to the Compound

My candle went out, and I could no longer write. Those last hours felt like a lifetime. The line of light coming from the salon was not enough to see much by. Kiya's sedative wore off, and she woke to near total darkness. How awful it must have been to wake up in such pain in a dark and strange place. "I'm here, Kiya," I said, whispering and hoping I could convince her to be quiet before she revealed our hiding place to everyone in the shop.

"Jasmina?"

"Yes, it's me. We have to whisper."

"It hurts."

"I know. We're going to get you to a doctor soon." I pleaded with God to make the sun set sooner.

"He said it wouldn't hurt much."

"He lied, Kiya. He was a monster."

She shifted and moaned. "Shh," I warned. I hated the idea of covering her mouth with my hand, but if I had to, I would do it. Too much was at stake. "Please, Kiya, we have to keep still and quiet."

"Where are we?"

"It's a very long story."

She moved again and sucked in a breath. "I'm not busy."

I sighed and reached over to feel her forehead again. It was burning hot.

"Tell me a story, Jasmina," she said. I heard pain in her voice. "Please."

Perhaps it would help distract her or at least keep her from talking. We sat in the dark, and I told her everything from the time she left for her operation until that moment. It was a long story, but not long enough. I looked through the small crack to see that dusk was falling. "We'll get help for you soon," I promised.

Finally the last customer left the salon, and Amrita's assistant pulled the long tin sliding door down across the entire front of the store, clicking it shut at her feet. I slid our door open and took in as much air as my lungs could hold. A match was lit, and the light revealed Amrita with a kerosene lantern in hand. She used the match to light the lantern and then turned to me. "There's a secret way to go out through the back. An auto will be waiting there for us."

"We need to hurry," I said. Kiya had gone mostly unconscious again, feverish and murmuring. "She will have to be carried."

"Wait here." Amrita came into our secret room and held the lantern up until she found a lever along the far wall. She pulled it, and a door opened. It took all three of us—Amrita, me, and the assistant—to get Kiya to the auto. Then we had to hold her on our laps so all of us would fit. After we rode down several streets, we turned a corner and the compound walls came into view. I nearly cried with relief.

"We're almost there, Kiya," I said. "Be strong. Help is near."

And it was. The guard at the gate had been standing outside, waiting for us, I think. We were not even to the gate when he opened it wide, and the auto drove inside. Amrita directed him to one of the buildings where several white people, more than I had seen in my entire life, waited out front.

The auto stopped, and Kiya was immediately taken from our arms into theirs. They carried her gently but quickly inside the building, the tallest man asking Amrita questions and then asking me when Amrita could not answer them. He ushered me inside while I told him about the operation, Kiya's wound, and her condition since.

He led me into a room where Kiya was already laid onto a small bed with her side exposed and the ugly slash across it a swollen, angry red. He looked at her and then directed his gaze to me. "I will do everything I can to save her life," he said to me, looking directly into my eyes, "but God is the Great Physician. Kiya's life is in His hands." Then he shocked me by taking my hand and with his other hand grasping Kiya's. I saw men and women all around the room join hands and lower their heads. The man, who I knew now to be the doctor, prayed for Kiya's life and her future, and for mine. He thanked God for delivering us from evil and asked God to guide his hands as he did surgery to remove the infection and repair what was damaged in Kiya's body. He asked that she live so she could hear about Jesus and how much God loved her.

I did not bow my head. I watched in awe as people nodded in agreement, their own lips moving in silent prayer on behalf of a stranger in need. A peace filled the room. It was not visible, but I could sense it all around me. How different this room was than the hospital room I had entered just that morning.

The doctor squeezed my hand after he finished praying. I was not sure what that gesture was meant to communicate, but his eyes communicated kindness. "You should go get some sleep," he said. "You can check on your friend in the morning."

I left the room and the building, unafraid for Kiya now that she had such gentle care.

It is now late, and I am in Grandmother's home again, Dapika having unearthed the key for me. She and Milo were outside when I left Kiya and wanted to know everything. It took a long time to tell them just a portion of it. Milo kept interrupting with questions or interjecting their part in the story from his perspective. In time Amrita emerged from the building and told me the doctor had to cut into Kiya's side again, but he was able to remove the dirty stitches and much of the infection, and Kiya should be improved by the morning. She then told us all to go to bed and left the compound. I wondered where her home was, or if she lived at the salon.

Dapika and Milo said good night and walked together to the orphanage building where they lived. I stared across the way to Grandmother's house, dreading going in. Grandmother was not there. Thankfully several days had to pass before her two weeks would be finished. I would be gone before then. Nevertheless, I still hesitated going inside. The house would be the same as I had left it, but I was changed, now so much older than the girl who had tried the shower or wondered about statues on shelves.

Fatigue finally moved me forward, and I went inside. I found a snack to eat in the refrigerator, drank a cooled bottle of water I had left behind and then sat down at the table to write this. Before I leave tomorrow, I will write a note for Grandmother to find when she returns, explaining that I will come back someday when I have earned the money to replace what I took. I will ask her to watch over Kiya for me, and I will tell her I am sorry.

First, however, I need to sleep.

Forty-one
The Light

Dear Mother,

I cannot believe all that has happened and must tell you about it. When I walked out of my room the next morning, my steps halted at the end of the hallway, my mind not believing what my eyes saw. "Grandmother!" She sat at the dining room table, this tattered, half-burned notebook open in her hands. At my exclamation, she held up a finger, which I had learned meant she wanted me to wait, and turned a page. I watched as she read to the last page I had written and then she closed the notebook and looked at me.

"Hello, Jasmina."

I could not speak for I was suddenly sobbing. I threw myself at her feet. "You aren't supposed to be back yet!" I cried. "The two weeks aren't over."

She pulled me up and wrapped her arms around me, rocking me as if I was a child. "Dear girl, you suggested two weeks away, not me. I took those girls home and visited my old village, and after a while I wanted to come home and see how you were doing. Oh, fiddlesticks." She chuckled at the English word. "Truth is these old bones cannot abide sleeping on the ground anymore."

She knew. She had read the notebook and knew everything. I poured out my remorse with my tears, telling her I would leave immediately to go begin earning the money back, but she stopped me with another hug, this one tighter. "You precious child. I forgive you, and Asha will forgive you too. Neither of us would want you to run off again to that evil world over money. The love of money causes all kinds of evil, as you have seen. I read your story, Jasmina. You made a big mistake, but it helped you understand your need for Jesus, and that is a very good thing."

Mother, she truly has forgiven me. Without forcing me to be her slave or someone else's slave until I repaid the debt, without a beating or a bribe. She says she will help me find you soon. This time, I will be glad of her presence, and definitely will not run away on my own ever again! I dream of the day you are set free, and I can tell you how giving my life to Jesus has filled me with a peace and joy such as I have never known. The Holy Book says God is my heavenly Father now, and in this I find great comfort. I had always hoped Father would come for us and save us, but he never cared enough to try. This heavenly Father did come for me. He rescued me and set me free, from the evil of others and the evil in myself, and I choose to be His forever.

For the first time in a long time, I am filled with hope. My friend Kiya will live, and for that I give thanks. Asha and Mr. Mark will return in a few weeks, and though I have forgiveness, I will still work to earn the money to replace what I took. It is the right thing to do. It will take less time than I had feared though, thanks to the international team. They came to see how Kiya was, and they told her they had confiscated a large stash of money when they arrested the men who came to pick up the organs. Part of that money belonged to Kiya, they said, for selling her kidney. They gave her a large sum, and then they gave a stack of rupee notes to me! I told them I still had both my kidneys, but they said it was payment for my help. I not only gave them information they had been seeking for many weeks—however unaware I was at the time—but I rescued all those girls from the basement and modeling agency and helped the team find and arrest the man who had trapped them there.

"You caught Gar?" I asked.

"He was a younger man and quite good looking."

"Fayeed." I was glad to think of him being put into jail, never able to torment and enslave anyone again, but if Gar was still out there, none of this was over. They did not find Gar or Samir, and I can only imagine Samir will seek to take Fayeed's place. I am afraid for him, for the darkness he has chosen.

As for me, I have experienced something beautiful and bright here in Grandmother's love and forgiveness for me, in the doctor and nurses' compassion for Kiya, and in how everyone accepted and welcomed me gladly, even after knowing the worst of who I am.

People tend to act like whatever god they follow. Because of these people, these followers of Jesus, I know God looks on me with true and unconditional and never-ending love. God has forgiven me and made me clean, like a newborn baby, innocent and without fault.

They have a word for it, Mother. It is called grace.

My immediate destiny remains unknown, but I no longer fear. God has given me a future and a hope. The trafficking will continue, but we will continue to fight it. And we will win with God's help, one person at a time.

Grandmother says that light always conquers darkness just as day follows night. I have emerged from a walk through more darkness than I thought existed. Now that I have found the light, I will never leave it. Someday I will find you, and you can walk into this light too.

Until that day, I love you, Mother. I miss you.

Your daughter forever,
Jasmina